Cathy Williams

The Wedding Night Debt

ISBN-13: 978-0-373-13378-9

Recycling programs for this product may not exist in your area.

The Wedding Night Debt

First North American Publication 2015

This edition published by arrangement with Harlequin Books S.A.

For questions and comments about the quality of this book, please contact us at CustomerService@Harlequin.com.

Printed in U.S.A.

"You want your divorce? You can have it. But only after you've given me what I expected to get when I married you."

"What are you talking about?"

Dio raised his eyebrows and smiled slowly. "Don't tell me that someone with a math degree can't figure out what two and two makes? I want my honeymoon, Lucy."

"I...I don't know what you mean..." Lucy stammered, unable to tear her eyes away from the harsh lines of his beautiful face.

"Of course you do. I didn't think I was signing up for a sexless marriage when I slipped that wedding band on your finger. You want out now? Well, you can have out just as soon as we put an end to the unfinished business between us."

"That's extortion!" She sprang to her feet. She had looked forward to that wretched honeymoon night so much...and now here he was, offering it to her...but at a price.

"That's the offer on the table. We sleep together, be man and wife in more than just name only, and you get to leave with an allowance generous enough to ensure that you spend the rest of your life in comfort."

"Why would you want that? You're not even attracted to me!"

"Come a little closer and I can easily prove you wrong on that point."

Heart thudding, Lucy noted the dark intent in his eyes, and the desire she had shoved away, out of sight, began to uncurl inside her.

Cathy Williams can remember reading Harlequin Presents books as a teenager, and now that she is writing them she remains an avid fan. For her, there is nothing like creating romantic stories and engaging plots, and each and every book is a new adventure. Cathy lives in London, and her three daughters—Charlotte, Olivia and Emma—have always been, and continue to be, the greatest inspirations in her life.

Books by Cathy Williams

Harlequin Presents

A Pawn in the Playboy's Game
At Her Boss's Pleasure
The Real Romero
The Uncompromising Italian
The Argentinian's Demand
Secrets of a Ruthless Tycoon
Enthralled by Moretti
His Temporary Mistress
A Deal with Di Capua
The Secret Casella Baby
The Notorious Gabriel Diaz
A Tempestuous Temptation

One Night With Consequences

Bound by the Billionaire's Baby

Seven Sexy Sins

To Sin with the Tycoon

Protecting His Legacy

The Secret Sinclair

Visit the Author Profile page
at Harlequin.com for more titles.

The Wedding Night Debt

To my three wonderful and inspiring daughters.

CHAPTER ONE

DIVORCE. IT WAS something that happened to other people: people who didn't take care of their marriages; who didn't understand that they were to be nurtured, looked after, handled as delicately as you would handle a piece of priceless porcelain.

At any rate, that had always been Lucy's way of thinking, and she wondered how it was that she was standing here now, in one of the grandest houses in London, waiting for her husband to return home so that she could broach the subject of divorcing him.

She looked at her diamond-encrusted watch and her stomach knotted in anxiety. Dio was due back in half an hour. She couldn't remember where he had spent the past week and a half. New York? Paris? They had places in both. Or maybe he had been in their Mustique villa. Maybe he had gone there with another woman. Who knew? She certainly didn't.

Self-pity threatened to engulf her and she stemmed the tide with ease of practice born of habit.

She'd been married for nearly a year and a half, plenty of time to get accustomed to the way her youthful dreams had crumbled to ashes.

When she glanced up, she could see herself reflected

in the huge, hand-made contemporary mirror which dominated the ultra-modern drawing room. Five foot ten, slender as a reed, long blonde hair that dropped to her shoulders, vanilla-blonde and poker-straight. When she was sixteen, she had been spotted by an agency and her father had tried to shove her into a career in modelling, because why waste a pretty face? After all, women weren't cut out for anything more challenging, not really… But she had resisted—not that it had done her any good at all, in the end, because what good had been her degree when she had ended up…here? In this vast house, wandering in and out of rooms like a wraith, playing the perfect hostess? As if perfect hostessing was any kind of career for someone who had a degree in maths.

She barely recognised the woman she had turned out to be. On a warm evening in the middle of July, she was languishing in silk culottes with a matching silk vest top, just a few discreet bits of fairly priceless jewellery and high heels. She had turned into a Stepford Wife, except without the adoring husband rolling in at five-thirty every evening and asking what was for dinner. That might have been a distinct improvement on what she actually had, which was…nothing.

Or, *had* been nothing. She allowed herself a little smile because things weren't quite as sterile as they had been. Her situation had changed in the past two months and she hugged that secret pleasure to herself.

It made up for all the time she had spent dressed up like an expensive doll, administering their various properties, smiling politely when she needed to smile politely and hosting dinner parties for the great and the good. Or, at any rate, the very, very rich.

And now…a divorce would set her free.

Provided Dio didn't kick up a fuss. Although she told herself that there was no reason for him to, she could still feel a prickle of nervous perspiration break out over her body.

When it came to the concrete jungle, Dio Ruiz was the pack leader. He was an alpha male who played by his own rules. He was the sexiest man on earth and also the most intimidating.

But he wasn't going to intimidate *her*. She had spent the past few days telling herself that, ever since she had decided which turning she would take at the crossroads—the turning that would put as much distance between herself and her husband as possible.

The only slight fly in the ointment was the fact that this would be the last thing he would be expecting and Dio didn't do well when it came to flies in the ointment, not to mention the unexpected.

She heard the slam of the front door and her stomach lurched sickeningly but she only turned around when she sensed him at the door, his powerful, restless personality permeating the room even before she looked at him.

Even now, after everything, hating him as much as she hated him, his physical beauty still managed to take her breath away.

At twenty-two, when she had first laid eyes on him, he had been the most sinfully stunning guy she had ever seen and nothing had changed on that front. He was still the most sinfully stunning guy she had ever seen. Raven-black hair framed arrogantly perfect features. His pale, silver-grey eyes, so unusual against his bronzed skin, were dramatically fringed with thick, dark lashes. His mouth was firm and sensuous. Every little bit of him relayed the message that he was not a guy to be messed with.

'What are you doing here? I thought you were in Paris…' Lounging in the doorway, Dio began tugging at his tie, strolling into the room at the same time.

Surprise, surprise. It wasn't often he found himself anywhere with his wife that hadn't been meticulously planned in advance. Their meetings were formal, staged, never, ever spontaneous. When they were both in London, their lives were hectic, a whirlwind of social events. They each had their separate quarters, readied themselves in their own private cocoons and met in the vast hall, both dressed to the nines and ready to present the united image that couldn't have been further from the truth.

Occasionally, she might accompany him to Paris, New York or Hong Kong, always the perfect accessory.

Smart, well-bred…and most of all stunningly beautiful.

Tie off, he tossed it onto the white leather sofa and circled her, frowning, before coming to rest directly in front of her, where he began undoing the top two buttons of his shirt.

'So…' he drawled. 'To what do I owe this unexpected pleasure?'

Her nostrils flared as she breathed him in. He had a scent that was peculiarly unique to him. Clean, woody and intensely masculine.

'Am I interrupting your plans for the evening?' She averted her eyes from the sliver of tanned chest just visible where he had unbuttoned the shirt.

'My plans involved reading through some fairly dull legal due diligence on a company I'm taking over. What plans did you think you might be interrupting?'

'No idea.' She shrugged her narrow shoulders. 'I don't know what you get up to in my absence, do I?'

'Would you like me to fill you in?'

'I don't care one way or another, although it might have been a little embarrassing if you'd come home with a woman on your arm.' She gave a brittle laugh, hating herself for how she sounded—hard, cold, dismissive.

It hadn't started out like this. In fact, she had actually been stupid enough, at the very beginning, to think that he was actually interested in her, actually attracted to her.

They had gone out on a few dates. She had made him laugh, telling him about some of her university friends and their escapades. She had listened, enthralled, about the places he had seen. The fact that her father had actually approved of the relationship had been a green light because her father had made a career out of disapproving of every single boy she had ever brought home, all three of them. In fact, he had made a career out of being critical and disapproving of everything she had ever done, and every choice she had ever made, so the fact that he had been accepting, *encouraging*, even, of Dio had been a refreshing change.

If she hadn't been so wet behind the ears, she might have asked herself why that was, but instead, heady with the joy of falling in love, she had chosen to overlook his sudden benevolence.

When Dio had proposed after a whirlwind romance she had been over the moon. The intense but chaste courtship had thrilled her, as had the fact that he hadn't wanted to wait. No long engagement for him! He had been eager to slip the ring on her finger and his eagerness had made her feel loved, wanted, desired.

Sometimes, she wondered whether she would have stupidly continued feeling loved, wanted and desired if she hadn't overheard that conversation on their wedding night. She'd been floating on a cloud, barely able to contain her excitement at the thought of their honeymoon in the Maldives and their wedding night, the big night when she would lose her virginity, because until then he had been the perfect gentleman.

He'd been nowhere to be seen and she had eventually floated away from the marquee in her father's garden, from the music and the people dancing and getting drunk, and had drifted off towards the kitchen and past her father's office, where she had immediately recognised the deep timbre of his voice.

A marriage of convenience…a company takeover… He had got her father's company, which had been losing money by the bucket load, and she had been an accessory thrown in for good measure. Or maybe, when she had bitterly thought about it later, her father had insisted on the marriage because if she was married to Dio he would remain duty-bound to the family company. No doing the dirty once the signatures had been written on the dotted line! No dumping her father in the proverbial because he was no longer an asset!

She would be her father's safety net and Dio—as her father had spitefully told her when she had later confronted him with what she had overheard—would get the sort of class that his vast sums of money would never have been able to afford him.

Lucy, in the space of a couple of hours, had grown up. She was a married woman and her marriage was over before she had even embarked on it.

Except, she couldn't get out of it, her father had told her, not that easily. Did she want to see the family company go under? There'd been some uncomfortable stuff with some of the company profits…a little borrowed here and there…he might go to prison if it all came out. Did she want that, to see her father behind bars? It would hit the news. Did she want that? Fingers pointed? People smirking?

She had acquiesced to her sham of a marriage although, frankly, her father might have escaped a prison sentence but only by handing the prison sentence over to her.

The one thing she had resolved, however, was to be married in name only. No sex. No cosy time together. If Dio thought that he had bought her body and soul, she had been determined to prove him wrong. When she thought of the way she had fallen for his charm, had thought he'd actually been interested in inexperienced little *her*, she had burned with shame.

So she had quietly put her dreams into a box, shut the lid and thrown away the key…and here she was now.

'Is there a problem with the Paris apartment?' Dio asked politely. 'Can I get you a drink? Something to celebrate the one-off occasion of us being in the same room alone without prior arrangement? I can't think of the last time that happened, can you?' But, at a push, he would have said before they'd got married, when she had been studiously courting him, even though at the time he had thought it to be the other way around.

He had set his sights on Robert Bishop and his company a long, long time ago. He had covertly kept tabs on it, had seen the way it had slid further and further into a morass of debt and, like any predator worth his salt, he had bided his time.

Revenge was always a dish best eaten cold.

He just hadn't banked on the daughter. One glimpse of Lucy and her innocent, ethereal beauty and he had altered his plans on the spot. He had wanted her. She had touched something in him with her innocence and, cynic that he was, he had fallen hook, line and sinker.

He hadn't banked on that complication, had thought that she would hop into bed with him, allowing him to get her out of his system before he concluded business with her father. But, after a few weeks of playing a courting game that wasn't his thing at all, he had concluded that he wanted more than just a slice of her.

Only thing was…nearly a year and a half later and their marriage was as dry as dust. He still hadn't touched that glorious body, leaving him with the certainty that, whilst he had thought he had the upper hand, she and her conniving father had actually played him for a fool. Instead of swinging the wrecking ball to the company and setting the police on Robert Bishop—who had been embezzling for years—he had ended up saving the company because he had wanted Lucy. He had wanted her at his side and in his bed and, if saving the company came as part of the deal, then so be it. Course, he had saved it and made money from it, ensuring that Robert Bishop was firmly locked out with just enough pocket money to teach him the joys of frugality, but still…

He had been unwittingly charmed by her open, shy, disingenuous personality. When she had looked at him with those big, grave brown eyes, her face propped in the palm of her hand, her expression enraptured, he had felt as though he had found the secret of eternal life and it had gone to his head like a drug.

She'd led him on. God knew if her slime of a father had kick-started the idea but that didn't matter.

What mattered was that they had got what they wanted

while he had certainly missed out on what *he* had banked on getting.

She was shaking her head at the offer of a drink and he ignored her, fetching himself a glass of whisky and a glass of wine for her.

'Relax,' he said, pressing the glass on her and then retreating to the bay window where he sipped his drink and watched her in absolute silence. She had made it crystal clear on their wedding night that theirs was not a real marriage. No sex, no chit-chat, no getting to know one another. So he'd taken over her father's company but that didn't mean that she came as part of the package deal and, if he thought he'd been short-changed, then that was too bad.

He hadn't asked how she knew, what her father had said or what she had been told. He'd been duped and that was the end of the story.

The thought of having any kind of soul-searching conversation about the quality of their marriage had never crossed Dio's mind. He had made no effort to talk things through. And no one could ever accuse her of not being the 'perfect wife'. She certainly looked the part. Willowy, blonde, with a devastating *prettiness* that conveyed an air of peculiar innocence underneath the polished exterior. It was a quality that no model or socialite could replicate. She looked like someone waiting for life to *happen* and people fell for it. She was the greatest business asset a man could have. The woman, Dio had often thought, had missed her career as an Oscar-winning actress.

'So, if you're not in Paris, it's because something's wrong with the apartment. You should know by now that I don't get involved with the nitty-gritty details of my houses. That's *your* job.'

Lucy stiffened. *Her* job. That said it all. Just what every young girl dreamed of…a marriage completely lacking in romance which could be described as a *job.*

'There's nothing wrong with the Paris apartment. I just decided that…' she took a deep breath and gulped down some wine '… I decided that we needed to have a talk…'

'Really? What about? Don't tell me that you're angling for a pay rise, Lucy? Your bank account is more than healthy. Or have you seen something you'd really like? House in Italy? Apartment in Florence? Buy it.' He shrugged and finished the remainder of his whisky. 'As long as it's somewhere that can be used for business purposes, then I don't have a problem.'

'Why would I want to buy a house, Dio?'

'What, then? Jewellery? A painting? What?'

His air of bored indifference set her teeth on edge. This was worse than normal. Usually, they could manage to be polite for the five minutes they were forced to spend in one another's company—cooped up in a taxi, maybe, or else waiting for his driver to take them to some opening or other; or else back in one of their grand houses, removing coats and jackets before disappearing to opposite ends of the house.

'I don't want to buy *anything*.' Restively she began walking, stopping to look absently at some of the expensive artefacts in the room. As with all their houses, this one was the last word in what money could buy. The paintings were breath-taking, the furniture was all handmade, the rugs were priceless silk.

No expense was ever spared and it was her *job* to ensure that all these high-end properties with their priceless furnishings ran like clockwork. Some were used by him, if he happened to be in the country at the time; occasionally they both found themselves in one at the same time. Often he arranged for clients to have use of them and then she had to oversee all the arrangements to make sure that his client left satisfied, having experienced the last word in luxury.

'In that case,' Dio drawled, 'why don't you get to the point and say what you have to say? I'm having a night in because I need to get through some work.'

'And of course, if you'd known that I would be waiting here like a spare part,' Lucy retorted, 'you would have made sure you didn't bother returning.'

Dio shrugged, allowing her to draw her own conclusions.

'I feel...' Lucy breathed in deeply '...that circumstances between us have changed since...since dad died six months ago...'

He stilled and dropped his empty glass on the side table next to him, although his silver-grey eyes remained on her face. As far as he was concerned, the world was a more pleasant place without Robert Bishop in it. Certainly a more honest one. Whether his wife would agree with him, he didn't know. She had been composed at the funeral, her eyes hidden behind over-sized sunglasses and, since then, life had carried on as normal.

'Explain.'

'I don't want to be shackled to you any more, and there's no longer any need.' She did her best to get her thoughts in order but the cool intensity of his gaze was off-putting.

'You also happen to be shackled to a lifestyle that most women would find enviable.'

'Then you should let me go and you should find one of those women,' she retorted, her cheeks burning. 'You'd be happier. I'm sure you would because you must know that I'm…not happy, Dio. Or maybe,' she added in a lowered voice, 'you do know and you just don't care.' She sat and crossed her legs but she couldn't meet his eyes. He still did things to her, could still make her feel squirmy inside, even though she had done her best over time to kill that weak feeling. It was inappropriate to be attracted to a man who had used you, who had married you because you happened to be a social asset. That didn't make sense. Yes, when he had pretended to be interested in her, she could understand how she had been hot for him, so hot that she had spent her nights dreaming about him and her days fantasising about him. But not when she had found out the truth, and certainly not now, after all this time of cold war.

'Are you telling me that you want out?'

'Can you blame me?' She answered a question with a question and finally met those cool, pale grey eyes. 'We don't have a marriage, Dio. Not a real one. I don't even understand why you married me in the first place, why you took an interest in me at all.' Except, of course, she did. Robert Bishop had been happy enough to tell her. Dio had wanted more than just his company; he had wanted social elevation, although why he should care she had no idea.

It was something she had never asked her husband. It was humiliating to think that someone had married you because you could open a few doors for them. She had been a bonus to the main deal because she had looked right and had had the right accent.

'You could have bought my father out without marrying me,' she continued, braving the iciness of his eyes. 'I know my father tried to shove me down your throat because he thought that, if you married me, he wouldn't end up in prison like a common criminal. But you could have had your pick of women who would have flung themselves in your path to be your wife.'

'How would you have felt if your dear daddy had ended up in jail?'

'No one wants to see any relative of theirs in prison.'

It was an odd choice of words but Dio let it go. He was shocked at the way this evening was turning out but he was hiding it well.

Had she really thought that she could play games with him, reel him in, get the ring on her, only to turn her back on his bed on their wedding night? And then, as soon as her father died, turn her back on him a second time?

'No, a relative in prison tends to blight family gatherings, doesn't it?' He rose to pour himself another drink because, frankly, he needed one. 'Tell me something, Lucy, what did you think of your father's...how shall I put it?...*creative use* of the company's pension pot?'

'He never told me in detail...what he had done,' she mumbled uncomfortably. Indeed, she had known nothing of her father's financial straits until that overheard conversation, after which he had been more than willing to fill her in.

Lucy thought that Dio might have been better off asking her what she had thought of her father. Robert Bishop had been a man who had had no trouble belittling her, a man who had wanted a son but had been stuck with a daughter, a chauvinist who had never accepted that women could be equal in all walks of life. Her poor, pretty, fragile mother had had a miserable existence before she had died at the tender age of thirty-eight. Robert Bishop had been a swaggering bully who had done his own thing and expected his wife to stay put and suck it up. He had womanised openly, had drunk far too much and, behind closed doors, had had fun jeering at Agatha Bishop, who had put up with it with quiet stoicism because divorce was not something her family did. Cancer had taken her before she'd been able to put that right.

Lucy had spent her life avoiding her father—which had been easy enough, because she had been farmed out to a boarding school at the age of thirteen—but she had never stopped hating him for what he put her mother through.

Which wasn't to say that she would have wanted to see him in prison and, more than that, she knew her mother would have been mortified. There was no way she would have sullied her mother's reputation, not if she could have helped it. She would rather have died than to have seen her mother's friends sniggering behind their backs that Agatha Bishop had ended up with a crook.

Looking at her, Dio wondered what was going through that beautiful head of hers. There was a remoteness there that had always managed to feed into his curiosity. No woman had ever been able to do that and it got on his nerves.

'Well, I'll fill in the gaps, shall I?' he said roughly. 'Your father spent years stealing from the pension fund until there was nothing left to steal. I assume he had a drinking problem?'

Lucy nodded. At boarding school and then university she had not had much time to observe just how much of a drinking problem he had had but it had been enough, she knew, to have sent his car spinning off the motorway at three in the morning.

'The man was an alcoholic. A functioning alcoholic,

bearing in mind he was crafty enough to get his greedy hands on other people's money, but the fact of the matter was that he nicked what didn't belong to him to the point that his entire company was destined to sink in the quicksand if I hadn't come along and rescued it.'

'Why did you?' she asked curiously. She assumed that he must have come from a working class background, if what her father had implied was true, but certainly, by the time he had crash-landed into her life, he was a self-made millionaire several times over. So why bother with her father's company?

Dio flushed darkly. Such a long and involved story and one he had no intention of telling her.

'It had potential,' he drawled, his beautiful mouth curving into a smile that could still make her heart beat a little faster. 'It had tentacles in all the right areas, and my intuition paid off. It's made me more money than I know what to do with. And then,' he continued softly, 'how many failing companies come with the added bonus of...*you?* Have you looked in the mirror recently, my darling wife? What red-blooded male could have resisted you? And your father was all too happy to close the deal and throw you in for good measure...'

He saw the way her face reddened and the way her eyes suddenly looked as though they were tearing up. For a split second, he almost regretted saying what he had said. *Almost.*

'Except,' he carried on in that same unhurried voice, 'I didn't get you, did I? You went out with me; you smiled shyly as you hung onto my every word; you let me get so close, close enough for me to need a cold shower every time I returned to my house, because you had turned retreating with a girlish blush into an art form... And then, on our wedding night, you informed me that you weren't going to be part of any deal that I had arranged. You led me on...'

'I... I...never meant to do that...' But she could see very clearly how the situation must have looked to a man like Dio.

'Now, I wonder why I find that so hard to believe?' he murmured, noticing with some surprise that he had finished his second drink. Regretfully, he decided against a third. 'You and your father concocted a little plan to make sure I was hooked into playing ball.'

'That's not true!' Bright patches of colour appeared on her cheeks.

'And then, once I had played ball, you were free to drop the act. So now you're talking about divorce. Your father's no longer in danger of the long arm of justice and you want out.' He tilted his head to one side as another thought crept in. For the first time, he wondered what she got up to in his many absences.

He could have put a tail on her but he had chosen not to. He had simply not been able to imagine his frozen ice-maiden doing anything behind his back. Except she hadn't always been that ice maiden, had she? There was more to her than that cool detachment. He had seen that for himself before she had said 'I do'... So *had* she been getting up to anything behind his back?

Was it a simple case of her wanting to divorce him, having given a sufficiently adequate period of mourning for her dear old daddy? Or was there some other reason lurking in the background...?

And, just like that, rage slammed into him with the force of a sledgehammer.

Had she been seeing some man behind his back? He

couldn't credit it but, once the nasty thought took hold, he found he couldn't jettison it.

'I want out because we both deserve something better than what we have.'

'How considerate of you to take my feelings into account.' Dio raised his eyebrows in a phoney show of gravity that made her grit her teeth. 'I never realised you had such a thoughtful, pious streak in you.'

First thing in the morning, he would have her followed, see for himself where this was all coming from. He certainly had no intention of asking her whether there was some guy in the background. In this sort of situation, nothing could beat the element of surprise.

'There's no need to be sarcastic, Dio.'

'Who's being sarcastic? Here's what I'm thinking, though...' He allowed a few seconds, during which time he pretended to give what was coming next some careful thought. 'You want out—but you do realise that you will leave with nothing?'

'What are you talking about?'

'I had a very watertight pre-nup made up before we married, which you duly signed, although I'm not entirely sure whether you read it thoroughly or not. My guess is that you were so eager to get me on board that signing anything would have just been a formality. Am I right?'

Lucy vaguely remembered signing something extremely long and complicated and very boring. She decided that she wouldn't take issue with his accusation that she'd been eager to get him on board; with his accusation that she had been in cahoots with her father to lure him into buying the company with her in the starring role of sacrificial lamb. She wasn't going to get involved in any sort of argument with him because he would emerge the winner. He had the sharpest brain of any person she had ever known in her life.

She would get out, never see him again. For a fleeting second, something wrenching and painful tugged inside her and she shoved the feeling away.

'As a rich man,' he said, 'I thought it best to protect myself. Here's what you signed up to. I got the company. Lock, stock and smoking barrel. Just recompense for rescuing it from imminent collapse and saving your father's frankly unworthy skin. I'm not sure if you know just how much he skimmed off the pension funds, how much I had to inject back in so that your employees didn't find themselves of pensionable age with nothing but a begging bowl for company? Enough for me to tell you that it was millions.' He breathed an exaggerated sigh and looked at her from under sinfully thick lashes. It had always amazed him that such a stupendously pretty face, so stunningly guileless, could house someone so cunning. It took all sorts to make the world.

Lucy hung her head because shame was never far away when her father's name was mentioned. She looked at her perfectly manicured nails and thought how wonderful it would feel never to wear nail polish ever again. She might have a burning-of-the-nail-polish ceremony.

She distractedly half-smiled and Dio, looking at her, frowned. So...what was the joke? he wondered.

More to the point, what was the little secret? Because that had been a secretive smile.

'As long as you are my wife,' he informed her, banking down the simmering rage bubbling up inside him, 'you get whatever you want. There are no limits placed on the amount of money you can spend.'

'You mean provided you approve of the purchases?'

'Have you ever heard me disapprove of anything you've ever bought?'

'All I buy are clothes, jewellery and accessories,' Lucy returned. 'And only because I need them to…play the part I have to play.'

'Your choice.' He shrugged. 'You could have bought a fleet of cars as far as I was concerned.'

She made a face and his frown deepened. He considered the possibility of giving her a divorce and dismissed the idea, although the reasons for that instant dismissal were a bit vague. Was he that possessive a man that he would hold on to a woman who wanted to escape? He had wanted revenge. And it might have come in a different shape from the one he had planned, but it had still come. He had still ended up with Robert Bishop's company, hadn't he? So what was the point of hanging on to Lucy and an empty marriage?

But then, she wasn't just any woman, was she? She just happened to be his wife. The wife who had promised a lot more than she had ended up delivering. What man liked being short-changed?

'You leave me,' he told her in a hard voice, 'and you leave with the clothes on your back.'

Lucy blanched. She loathed the trappings of wealth but wasn't it a fact that that was all she had ever known? How would she live? What sort of job had years of being pampered prepared her for? She had never had the opportunity to do the teacher training course she had wanted to do. She had, instead, jumped into a marriage that had turned her into a clone of someone she didn't like very much.

'I don't care,' she said in a low voice and Dio raised his eyebrows in a question.

'Of course you do,' he told her. 'You wouldn't know where to begin when it came to finding a job.'

'You can't say that.'

'Of course I can. You've grown up in the lap of luxury and, when most other girls would have branched out into the big, bad world, you married me and continued your life of luxury. Tell me, what has prepared you for that ugly, grim thing called reality?'

He would turf her out without a penny. She could see that in his eyes. He had never cared a jot about her and he didn't care about her now. He had wanted the company and she had been a useful tool to acquire along with the bricks and mortar.

She just recently might have dipped her toe in that grim thing he was talking about called reality, but he was right. A life of creature comforts hadn't prepared her for striking out with nothing. It would take ages for her to find her feet in the world of work, and how would she survive in the meantime? When he told her that she would leave with nothing but the clothes on her back, she was inclined to believe him. The clothes on her back wouldn't include the expensive jewellery in the various safes and vaults.

'I can see that you know where I'm coming from…' He leaned forward, arms resting loosely on his thighs. 'If you want out, then you have two options. You go with nothing, or…'

Lucy looked at him warily. 'Or…what?'

CHAPTER TWO

DIO SMILED SLOWLY and relaxed back.

Sooner or later, this weird impasse between them would have had to find a resolution; he had known that. Always one to dominate the situations around him, he had allowed it to continue for far longer than acceptable.

Why?

Had he thought that she would have thawed slowly? She'd certainly shown no signs of doing anything of the sort as the months had progressed. In fact, they had achieved the unthinkable—a functioning, working relationship devoid of sex, a business arrangement that was hugely successful. She complemented him in ways he could never have imagined. She had been the perfect foil for his hard-nosed, aggressive, seize-and-conquer approach to business and, frankly, life in general. He hadn't been born with a silver spoon in his mouth, he had had to haul himself up by his boot straps, and the challenges of the journey to success had made him brutally tough.

He was the king of the concrete jungle and he was sharp enough to know that pretenders to the throne were never far behind. He was feared and respected in equal measure and his wife's ingrained elegance counterbalanced his more high-voltage, thrusting personality beautifully.

Together they worked.

Maybe that was why he had not broached the subject of all those underlying problems between them. He was a practical man and maybe he had chosen not to rock the boat because they had a successful partnership.

Or maybe he had just been downright lazy. Or—and this was a less welcome thought—vain enough to imagine that the woman he still stupidly fancied would end up coming to him of her own accord.

The one thing he hadn't expected was talk of a divorce.

He poured himself another drink and returned to the chair, in no great hurry to break the silence stretching between them.

'When we got married,' Dio said slowly, 'it didn't occur to me that I would end up with a wife who slept in a separate wing of the house when we happened to be under the same roof. It has to be said that that's not every man's dream of a happy marriage.'

'I didn't think you had dreams of happy marriages, Dio. I never got the impression that you were the sort of guy who had fantasies of coming home to the wife and the two-point-two kids and the dog and the big back garden.'

'Why would you say that?'

Lucy shrugged. 'Just an impression I got.' But that hadn't stopped her from falling for him. She had got lost in those amazing eyes, had been seduced by that deep, dark drawl and had been willing to ignore what her head had been telling her because her heart had been talking a lot louder.

'I may not have spent my life gearing up for a walk

down the aisle but that doesn't mean that I wanted to end up with a woman who didn't share my bed.'

Lucy reddened. 'Well, both of us has ended up disappointed with what we got,' she said calmly.

Dio waved his hand dismissively. 'There's no point trying to analyse our marriage,' he said. 'That's a pointless exercise. I was going to talk to you about options…' He sipped his drink and looked at her thoughtfully. 'And I'm going to give you a very good one. You want a divorce? Fine. I can't stop you heading for the nearest lawyer and getting divorce papers drawn up. Course, like I said, that would involve you leaving with nothing. A daunting prospect for someone who has spent the last year and a half never having to think about money.'

'Money isn't the be all and end all of everything.'

'Do you know what? It's been my experience that the people who are fond of saying things like that are the people who have money at their disposal. People who have no money are usually inclined to take a more pragmatic approach.' Having grown up with nothing, Dio knew very well that money actually was the be all and end all of everything. It gave you freedom like nothing else could. Freedom to do exactly what you wanted to do and to be accountable to no one.

'I'm saying that it doesn't always bring happiness.' She thought of her own unhappy, lavish childhood. From the outside, they had looked like a happy, privileged family. Behind closed doors, it had been just the opposite. No amount of money had been able to whitewash that.

'But a lack of it can bring, well, frustration? Misery? Despair? Imagine yourself leaving all of this so that you can take up residence in a one-bedroom flat where you'll live a life battling rising damp and mould on the walls.'

Lucy gave an exaggerated sigh. 'Aren't you being a bit dramatic, Dio?'

'London is an expensive place. Naturally, you would have some money at your disposal, but nothing like enough to find anywhere halfway decent to live.'

'Then I'd move out of London.'

'Into the countryside? You've lived in London all your life. You're accustomed to having the theatre and the opera and all those art exhibitions you enjoy going to on tap… But don't worry. You can still enjoy all of that but, sadly, there's no such thing as a free lunch. You want your divorce? You can have it. But only after you've given me what I expected to get when I married you.'

It took a few seconds for Lucy's brain to make the right connections and catch up with what he was telling her but, even so, she heard herself ask, falteringly, 'What are you talking about?'

Dio raised his eyebrows and smiled slowly. 'Don't tell me that someone with a maths degree can't figure out what two and two makes? I want my honeymoon, Lucy.'

'I… I don't know what you mean…' Lucy stammered, unable to tear her eyes away from the harsh lines of his beautiful face.

'Of course you do! I didn't think I was signing up for a sexless marriage when I slipped that wedding band on your finger. You want out now? Well, you can have out just as soon as we put an end to the unfinished business between us.'

'That's blackmail!' She sprang to her feet and began restively pacing the room. Her nerves were all over the place. She had looked forward to that wretched honeymoon night so much…and now here he was, offering it to her, but at a price.

'That's the offer on the table. We sleep together, be man and wife in more than just name only, and you get to leave with an allowance generous enough to ensure that you spend the rest of your life in comfort.'

'Why would you want that? You're not even attracted to me!'

'Come a little closer and I can easily prove you wrong on that point.'

Heart thudding, Lucy kept a healthy distance, but she was looking at him again, noting the dark intent in his eyes. The desire she had shoved away, out of sight, began to uncurl inside her.

She'd been foolish enough to think that he had been interested in her, attracted to her, and had discovered that it had all been a lie. He had strung her along because he had decided that she would be a useful addition to his life.

There was no way that she would sleep with him as some sort of devil's bargain. She had watched the car crash of her parents' marriage and had vowed that she would only give her body to a man who truly loved her, that she would only marry for the right reasons. Her parents had had a marriage of convenience, the natural joining of two wealthy families, and just look at where they had ended up. The minute she had realised that her marriage to Dio had not been what she had imagined was the minute she'd made her decision to withhold the better part of herself from him, to remain true to her principles.

She watched, horrified, as he slowly rose from his chair and strolled towards where she was standing by the window. With each step, her nerves shredded a little bit more.

'A matter of weeks…' he murmured, delicately tracing his finger along her cheek and feeling her quiver as he touched her.

She was the only woman in the world he had never been able to read.

There had been times during their marriage when he had surprised her looking at him, had seen something in her eyes that had made him wonder whether his dear wife was slightly less immune to him than she liked to portray, but he had never explored the possibility. There was such a thing as pride, especially to a man like him.

He was willing to explore the possibility now because he knew that, if she left and he never got to touch her, she would become unfinished business and that would be a less than satisfactory outcome.

'Weeks…?' Transfixed by the feel of his skin against hers, Lucy remained rooted to the spot. Her breasts ached and she could feel her nipples tightening, sensitive against her lacy bra. Liquid was pooling between her legs and, although she remained perfectly still, she wanted to squirm and rub her legs together to relieve herself of the ache between them.

'That's right.' Plenty long enough to get her out of his system. She was his and he intended to have her, all of her, before he allowed her her freedom.

At which point, he would close the door on a part of his past that had gnawed away at him for as long as he could remember.

His erection was hard enough to be painful and he stepped a bit closer, close enough for her to feel it against her belly. He knew that she had from the slight shudder that ran through her body. Her eyes were wide, her mouth parted.

An invitation. One that he wasn't going to resist. He

hadn't been this physically close to his wife since he had tied the knot with her and he wasn't about to waste the opportunity.

Lucy knew he was going to kiss her. She placed her hand flat on his chest, a pathetic attempt to push him away before he could get too close, but she didn't push him away. Instead, as his mouth found hers, treacherous fingers curled into his shirt and she sighed, losing herself in the headiness of feeling his tongue probing into her mouth, his tongue moving, exploring, with hers, sparking a series of explosive reactions in her body.

Like a match set to tinder, she felt her whole body combusting. Their brief courtship had been so very chaste. This wasn't chaste. This was unrestrained hunger and his hunger matched her own.

She felt him slip his hand underneath the silk top to cup her breast and, when he began to rub her nipple through the lacy bra, she wanted to pass out.

Or else rip off his shirt so that she could spread trembling, eager fingers against his broad, hard chest.

He pulled back. It took her a couple of seconds to recognise his withdrawal and then horror at what she had allowed to happen filtered through her consciousness and washed over her like a bucket of freezing cold water.

'What the heck do you think you're doing?'

Dio smiled. 'Giving you proof positive that we could have a couple of weeks of very pleasant carnal adventures…' Keen eyes noted the hectic flush in her cheeks and the way she had now prudishly folded her arms across her chest, as if she could deny the very heated, very satisfactory, response she had just given him.

He hadn't been mistaken when it came to those little looks he had surprised her giving him after all.

'I have no intention of…of sleeping with you for money!'

Dio's lips thinned. 'Why not? You married me for money. At least sleeping with me would introduce the element of fun.'

'I did not marry you for money!'

'I have no intention of going down this road again. I've given you your options. You can decide which one to go for.' He spun round on his heels, heading for the door.

'Dio!'

He stilled and then took his time turning to face her.

'Why?'

'Why what?'

'Why does it matter whether you sleep with me or not? I mean surely there have been…women in your life over the past year or so more than willing to jump into bed with you… Why does it matter whether I do or not?'

Dio didn't answer immediately. He knew what she thought, that he spent his leisure time between the sheets with other women. There had been no need for her to vocalise it. He had seen it in her face on the few occasions when he had happened to be in conversation with another woman, an attractive woman. He had seen the flash of resentment and scorn which had been very quickly masked and he had seen no reason to put her straight.

He didn't think that there was any need to put her straight now. Not only had he not slept with any other woman since his marriage, but he had not been tempted. There wasn't a human being on earth who wasn't driven to want what was out of reach and his wife had been steadfastly out of reach for the past eighteen months. During that period, he had not found his eyes straying to any of the women who had covertly made passes at him over the months, happy to overlook the fact that there was a wedding ring on his finger.

'I just can't,' Lucy breathed into the silence. 'I… I'm happy to leave with a small loan, until I find my feet.'

'Find your feet doing what?' Dio asked curiously.

'I… I have one or two things up my sleeve…'

Dio's eyes narrowed as hers shifted away. He was picking up the whiff of a secret and he wondered, again, what was going on behind his back. What *had* been going on behind his back? Had the mouse been playing while the cat had been away?

'What things?'

'Oh, nothing,' she said evasively. 'It's just that… I think we'd both be happier if we brought this marriage to an end, and if I could borrow some money from you…'

'Lucy, you would need a great deal of money to begin to have any life at all in London.'

'Money which you are not at all prepared to lend me, even though you have my word that you would be repaid.'

'Unless you're planning a big job in the corporate world or have a rich backer,' he said dryly, 'then I can guarantee that any loan I make to you would not be paid back. At least, not while I have my own teeth and hair.'

'How do you think it would look if your wife was caught with a begging bowl, looking for scraps from strangers?'

'Now who's being dramatic?' When he had met her all those months ago, she had been blushing and shy but he had had glimpses of the humour and sharp intelligence behind the shyness. Over the past year and a half, as she had been called on to play the role of perfect wife and accomplished hostess, her self-confidence had grown in leaps and bounds.

He also knew that, whatever she felt for him, she wasn't intimidated by him. Maybe that, too, was down to the strange configuration of their lives together. How could you be intimidated by someone you weren't that interested in pleasing in the first place?

'You will, naturally, walk away with slightly more than the clothes on your back,' Dio admitted. 'However, you would still find it a challenge to have a lifestyle that in any way could be labelled comfortable. Unless, of course, there's a rich patron in the background. Is there?'

Asking the question was a sign of weakness but Dio couldn't help himself.

She shrugged. 'I'm not into rich men,' she told him. 'I've always known that and having been married to you has confirmed all my suspicions.'

'How's that?' Frankly, he had never heard anything so hypocritical in his life before, but he decided to let it pass.

'Like you said, there's no such thing as a free lunch. I know you say that it's the most important thing in life…'

'I can't remember saying that.'

'More or less. You said it *more or less*. And I know you think that I wouldn't be able to last a week unless I have more money than I can shake a stick at but—'

'But you're suddenly overcome with a desperate urge to prove me wrong…' His gaze dropped to her full mouth. Something about the arrangement of her features had always turned him on. She wasn't overtly sexy, just as she wasn't overtly beautiful, but there was a whisper of something other-worldly about her that kept tugging his eyes back to her time and time again.

She had screwed up his clear-cut plans to buy her father's company at a fire sale price before chucking him to his fate, which would undoubtedly have involved wolves tearing him to pieces. He had been charmed by that other-worldly *something*, had allowed it somehow to get to him, and he had tempered all his plans to accommodate the feeling.

She had, over time, become the itch he couldn't scratch. He might have had her signed up to a water-tight pre-nup but, even so, he would never have seen her hit the streets without any financial wherewithal.

In this instance, though, he was determined to have that itch scratched and, if it meant holding her to ransom, then he was pretty happy to go down that road.

Especially now that he knew that the attraction was returned in full.

'I'm just trying to tell you that there's no rich any-one in the background.' Did he imagine that she fooled around the way he did? 'And there never will be anyone rich in my life again.'

'How virtuous. Is it because of those free lunches not coming for free? Do you honestly think that hitching your life to a pauper would be fertile ground for happily united bliss? If so then you really need to drag your head out of the clouds and get back down to Planet Earth.' He abandoned the decision to go back to work, not that he would have been able to concentrate. 'I don't know about you, but I'm hungry. If we're going to continue this con-versation, then I need to eat.'

'You were about to leave,' Lucy reminded him.

'That was before I became intrigued with your radi-cal new outlook on life.'

He began heading towards the kitchen and she fol-lowed helplessly in his wake.

This felt like a proper conversation and it was unset-tling. There were no crowds of people around jostling for his attention. No important clients demanding polite small talk. And they weren't exchanging pleasantries before heading off in opposite directions in any one of their grand houses.

She knew the layout of the kitchen well. On those occasions when they had entertained at home, she had had to supervise caterers and familiarise them with the ins and outs of the vast kitchen. When he was out of the country, as he often was, this was where she had her meals on her own, with the little telly on, or else the radio.

However, it was a bit different to see him here, in it.

For a few seconds, he stared around him, a man at sea trying to get his bearings.

'Okay. Suggestions?' He finally turned to her.

'Suggestions about what?'

'Thoughts on what I can eat.'

'What were you planning to eat if you hadn't found me here?' Lucy asked jerkily, moving from doorway to kitchen table and then sitting awkwardly on one of the chairs while he continued to look at her in a way that made her blood sizzle, because she just had to see that mouth of his to recall his very passionate kiss. Her lips still felt stung and swollen.

'I have two top chefs on speed dial,' he drawled, amused when her mouth fell open. 'They're usually good at solving the "what to eat?" dilemma for me. Not that it's a dilemma that occurs very often. If I'm on my own, I eat out. Saves hassle.'

'Go ahead and order what you want from your two top chefs,' Lucy told him. 'Never mind me. I…er…'

'Ate already?'

'I'm not hungry.'

'And I don't believe you. Don't tell me,' he said, 'that

you feel uncomfortable being in a kitchen with me and breaking bread? We're a married couple, after all.'

'I don't feel uncomfortable,' Lucy lied. 'Not in the slightest!'

'Then where are your suggestions?'

'Do you even know where to find anything in this kitchen?' she asked impatiently.

Dio appeared to give that question a bit of thought then he shook his head. 'I admit the contents of the cupboards are something of a mystery, although I do know that there's some very fine white wine in the fridge…'

'Are you asking me to cook something for you?'

'If you're offering, then who am I to refuse?' He made for a chair and sat down. 'It doesn't offend your feminist instincts to cook for me, does it? Because, if it does, then I'm more than happy to try and hunt down one or two ingredients and put my cooking skills to the test.'

'You don't have cooking skills.' From some past remembered conversation, when she had still had faith in him, she recalled one of his throwaway remarks that had made her laugh.

'You're right. So I don't.'

This wasn't how Lucy had imagined the evening going. She had more figured on dealing with shock at her announcement followed by anger because she knew that, even if he heartily wanted to get rid of her, he would have been furious that she had pre-empted him. Then she had imagined disappearing off to bed, leaving him to mull over her decision, at which point she would have been directed to a lawyer who would take over the handling of the nitty-gritty.

Instead she felt trapped in the eye of a hurricane…

She knew where everything was and she was a reasonably good cook. It was something she quite enjoyed doing when she was on her own, freed from the pressure of having to entertain. She expertly found the things she needed for a simple pasta meal and it would have been relaxing if she hadn't been so acutely aware of his eyes following her every movement.

'Need a hand?' he asked as she clanged a saucepan onto the stove and she turned to him with a snappy, disbelieving frown.

'What can you do?'

'I feel I could be quite good at chopping things.' He rose smoothly to join her by the kitchen counter, invading her space and making her skin tingle with sexual awareness.

Stupid, she thought crossly. But he had thrown down that gauntlet, brought sex into the equation, and now it was on her mind. And she didn't want it to be. She had spent the past months telling herself that she hated him and hating him had made it easy for her to ignore the way he made her feel. It had been easy to ignore the slight tremble whenever he got too close, the tingling of her breasts and the squirmy feeling she got in the pit of her stomach.

He'd never been attracted to her, she had thought. He'd just seen her as part of a deal. He'd used her.

But now…

He wanted her; she had felt it in his kiss, had felt his erection pressing against her like a shaft of steel. Just thinking about it brought her out in a fine film of perspiration.

She shoved an onion and some tomatoes at him and told him where to find a chopping board and a knife.

'Most women would love the kind of lifestyle you

have,' Dio murmured as he began doing something and nothing with the tomatoes.

'You mean flitting from grand house to grand house, making sure everything is ticking over, because Lord help us if an important client spots some dust on a skirting board?'

'Since when have you been so sarcastic?'

'I'm not being sarcastic.'

'Don't stop. I find it intriguing.'

'You told me that most women would envy what I have and I told you that they wouldn't.'

'You'd be surprised what women would put up with if the price was right.'

'I'm not one of those women.' She edged away, because he was just a little too close for comfort, and began busying herself by the stove, flinging things into the saucepan, all the ingredients for a tomato-and-aubergine dish, which was a stalwart in her repertoire because it was quick and easy.

Dio thought that maybe he should have tried to find out what sort of woman she was before remembering that he knew exactly what sort of woman she was. The sort who had conspired with her father to get him where they had both wanted him—married to her and thereby providing protection for her father from the due processes of law.

If she wanted to toss out hints that there were hidden depths there somewhere, though, then he was happy enough to go along for the ride. Why not? Right now he was actually enjoying himself, against all odds.

And the bottom line was that he wanted her body. He wanted that itch to be scratched and then he would be quite happy to dispose of her.

If holding her to ransom was going to prove a problem then what was the big deal in getting her into his bed using other methods?

'So, we're back to the money not being the be all and end all,' he murmured encouragingly. 'Smells good, whatever you're making.'

'I like cooking when I'm on my own,' she said with a flush of pleasure.

'You cook even though you know you could have anything you wanted to eat delivered to your doorstep?' Dio asked with astonishment and Lucy laughed.

He remembered that laugh from way back when. Soft and infectious, with a little catch that made it seem as though she felt guilty laughing at all. He had found that laugh strangely seductive, fool that he had been.

'So…' he drawled once they were sitting at the kitchen table with bowls of steaming hot pasta in front of them. 'Shall we raise our glasses to this rare event? I don't believe I've sat in this kitchen and had a meal with you since we got married.'

Lucy nervously sipped some of the wine. The situation was slipping away from her. How many women had he sat and drank with in the time during which they had been supposedly happily married? She hadn't slept with him but that didn't mean that she wasn't aware that he had a healthy libido. One look at that dark, handsome face was enough to cement the impression.

She had never, not once, asked him about what he did behind her back on all those many trips when he was abroad, but she could feel the questions eating away at her, as though they had suddenly been released from a locked box. She hated it. And she hated the way that fleeting moment of being the object of his flirting attention had got to her, overriding all the reasons she had formulated in her head for breaking away from him. She didn't want to give house room to any squirmy feelings. He had turned on the charm when they had first met and she knew from experience that it didn't mean anything.

'That's because this isn't really a marriage, is it?' she said politely. 'So why would we sit in a kitchen and have a meal together? That's what real married couples do.'

Dio's mouth tightened. 'And of course you would know a lot about what real married couples do, considering you entered this contract with no intention of being half of a real married couple.'

'I don't think it's going to get either of us anywhere if we keep harping back to the past. I think we should both now look to the future.'

'The future being divorce.'

'I'm not going to get into bed with you for money, Dio,' Lucy told him flatly. For a whisper of a second, she had a vivid image of what it would be like to make love to him—but then, it wouldn't be love, would it? And what was the point of sex without love?

'So you're choosing the poverty option.' He pushed his bowl to one side and relaxed back in the chair, angling his big body so that he could extend his legs to the side.

'If I have to. I can make do. I…'

'You…what?' His ears pricked up as he detected the hesitancy in her voice.

'I have plans,' Lucy said evasively. And she wasn't going to share them with him, wasn't going to let her fledgling ambitions be put to the test by him.

'What plans?'

'Nothing very big. Or important. I just obviously need to think about the direction my life is going in.' She stood up and briskly began clearing the table. She made sure not to catch his eye.

Dio watched her jerky movements as she busied herself around the kitchen, tidying, wiping the counters, doing everything she could to make sure the conversation was terminated.

So she wanted out and she had plans.

To Dio's way of thinking, that could only mean one thing. A man. Maybe not a rich one, but a man. Lurking in the background. Waiting to get her into bed if he hadn't already done so.

The fake marriage was going to be replaced by a relationship she had probably been cultivating behind his back for months. Maybe—and the red mist descended when he considered this option—she had been cultivating this relationship from way back when. Maybe it had been right there on the back burner, set to one side while she'd married him and had done what she had to do for the sake of her father.

It might have come as a shock that she would face walking away empty handed but clearly, whatever her so-called plans were, they were powerful enough to override common sense.

Faced with this, Dio understood that first and foremost he would find out what those plans were.

Simple.

He could either follow her himself or he could employ someone to do it. He preferred the former option. Why allow someone else to do something you were perfectly capable of handling yourself?

The past year or so of their sterile non-relationship faded under the impetus of an urgent need that obliterated everything else.

'I'm going to be in New York for the next few days,' Dio said abruptly, standing up and moving towards the kitchen door where he stood for a few seconds, hand on the door knob, his dark face cool and unreadable. 'While you're still wearing a wedding ring on your finger, I could insist that you accompany me, because I will be attending some high level social events. But, under these very *special* circumstances, you'll be pleased to hear that I won't.'

'New—New York?' Lucy faltered. 'I can't remember New York being in the diary until next month…'

'Change of plan.' Dio shrugged. He stared at her, working out what he planned to do the following day and how. 'You can stay here and spend the time thinking about the proposition I've put to you.'

'I've already thought about it. I don't need to do any more thinking.'

Over his dead body. 'Then,' he said smoothly, 'you can stay here and spend the time contemplating the consequences…'

CHAPTER THREE

LUCY HAD HAD better nights.

Spend her time contemplating the consequences? The cool, dismissive way he had said that, looking at her as if he had complete authority over her decisions, had set her teeth on edge.

Their sham of a marriage had worked well for him. She knew that. Her father had told her that Dio wanted someone classy to be by his side and she had fitted the bill. Whilst he had been alive, he had never ceased reminding her that it was her duty to play the part because, if she didn't, then it would be within her husband's power to reveal the extent of the misappropriated money—and if he went down, her father had told her, then so too would the memory of her mother. The dirty linen that would be washed in public would bring everyone down. That was how it worked.

That had been Lucy's Achilles' heel so she had played her part and she had played it to perfection.

The day after their wedding, Dio had taken himself off to the other side of the world on business and, during the week that he had been away, she had obeyed instructions and had overhauled her image with the aid of a top-notch personal shopper.

Like a puppet, she had allowed herself to be manoeuvred into being the sort of woman who entertained. He had returned and there and then the parameters of their personal life had been laid down.

He had said nothing about her physical withdrawal. The closeness that had been there before her father's revelation had disappeared, replaced by a cool remoteness that had only served to prove just how right she had been in reading the situation.

He had used her.

What he had wanted was what he had got. He had wanted someone to whom the social graces came as second nature. He mixed in the rarefied circles of the elite and she could more than hold her own in those circles because she had grown up in them.

As far as she knew, the sort of woman he was attracted to was probably completely the opposite to her.

He was probably attracted to dark-haired, voluptuous sirens who didn't hang around the house in silk culottes and matching silk vests. He probably liked them swearing, cursing and being able to drink him under the table, but none of *them* would have done as a society wife. So he had tacked her on as a useful appendage.

And now he wanted her.

With divorce on the horizon, he wanted to lay claim to her because, as far as he was concerned, she was his possession, someone he had bought along with the company that had come with her.

He'd even set a time line on whatever physical relationship he intended to conduct!

Did it get any more insulting?

He knew that he'd be bored with her within a month!

She burned with shame when she thought about that.

She hated him and yet her sleep was disturbed by a series of images of them together. She dreamt of him making love to her, touching her in places she had never been touched before and whispering things in her ear that had her squirming in a restless half-sleep.

She awoke the following morning to an empty house. Dio had disappeared off to New York.

She'd used these little snippets of freedom to her benefit and now, as she got dressed, she felt that she should be a little more excited than she was.

It irritated her to know that, thanks to Dio, the glorious day stretching ahead of her was already marred with images of his dark, commanding face and the careless arrogance of what he had told her the evening before.

She made a couple of calls and then she headed out.

Dio, in the middle of a conference call, was notified of her departure within seconds of her leaving the house.

His personal driver—who had zero experience in sleuthing but could handle a car like a pro and could be trusted with his life—phoned the message through and Dio immediately terminated his conference call.

'When she stops, call me,' he instructed. 'I'm not interested in whether she's leaving the house. I'm interested in where she ends up.'

Suddenly restless, he pushed himself away from his desk and walked towards the floor-to-ceiling glass panes that overlooked the busy hub of the city.

He'd had a night to think about what she had told him and he was no nearer to getting his head around it.

So, she wanted out.

She was the single one woman who had eluded him despite the ring on her finger. To take a protesting bride to his bed would have been unthinkable. There was no way he would ever have been driven to that, however bitter he might have been about the warped terms of their marriage. And he could see now that pride had entered the equation, paralysing his natural instinct to charm her into the place he wanted her to be.

With the situation radically changed, it was time for him to be proactive.

And he was going to enjoy it. He was going to enjoy having her beg for him, which he fully intended she would do, despite all her protests to the contrary.

And, if he discovered that there was a man on the scene, that she had been seeing someone behind his back…

He shoved his hands in his pockets and clenched his jaw, refusing to give in to the swirl of fury that filled every pore and fibre of his being at the thought of her possible infidelity.

When he had embarked on Robert Bishop's company buyout, this was not at all what he had envisaged.

He had envisaged a clean, fatal cut delivered with the precision of a surgical knife, which was no less than the man deserved.

Never one to waste time brooding, Dio allowed his mind to play back the series of events that had finally led to the revenge he had planned so very carefully.

Some of what he had known, he had seen with his own eyes, growing up. His father fighting depression, stuck in a nowhere job where the pay was crap. His mother working long hours cleaning other people's houses so that there would be sufficient money for little treats for him.

The greater part of the story, however, had come from his mother's own lips, years after his father's life had been claimed by the ravages of cancer. Only then had he discovered the wrong that had been done to his father. A poor immigrant with a brilliant mind, he had met Robert Bishop as an undergraduate. Robert Bishop, from all accounts, had been wasting his time partying whilst pretending to do a business degree. Born into money, but with the family fortunes already showing signs of poor health, he had known that although he had an assured job with the family business he needed more if he was to sustain the lifestyle to which he had become accustomed.

Meeting Mario Ruiz had been a stroke of luck as far as Robert Bishop had been concerned. He had met the genius who would later invent something small but highly significant that would allow him to send his ailing family engineering concern into the stratosphere.

And as for Mario Ruiz?

Dio made no attempt to kill the toxic acid that always erupted in his veins when he thought of how his father had been conned.

Mario Ruiz had innocently signed up to a deal that had not been worth the paper it was written on. He had found his invention misappropriated and, when he had raised the issue, had found himself at the mercy of a man who'd wanted to get rid of him as fast as he could.

He had seen nothing of all the giddy financial rewards that should have been his due.

It had been such an incredible story that Dio might well have doubted the full extent of its authenticity had it not been for the reams of paperwork later uncovered after his mother had died, barely months after his father had been buried.

Ruining Robert Bishop had been there, driving him

forward, for many years…except complete and total revenge had been marred by the fresh-faced, seductive prettiness of Lucy Bishop. He had wavered. Allowed concessions to be made. Only to find himself the revenge half-baked: he had got the company but not the man, and he had got the girl but not in the way he had imagined he would.

Well, he just couldn't wait to see how this particular story was going to play out. Not on her terms, he resolved.

He picked up the call from his driver practically before his mobile buzzed and listened with a slight frown of puzzlement as he was given his wife's location.

Striding out of his office, he said in passing to his secretary that he would be uncontactable for the next couple of hours.

He wasn't surprised to see the look of open-mouthed astonishment on his secretary's face because, when it came to work, he was *always* contactable.

'Make up whatever excuses you like for my cancelled meetings, be as inventive as the mood takes you.' He grinned, pausing by the door. 'You can look at it as your little window of living dangerously…'

'I live dangerously every time I walk through that office door,' his austere, highly efficient, middle-aged secretary tartly responded. 'You have no idea what you're like to work for!'

Dio knew the streets of London almost as comprehensively as his driver did but he still had to rely on his satnav to get him to the address he had been given.

Somewhere in East London. He had no idea how Jackson had managed to follow Lucy. Presumably, he had just taken whatever form of public transport she had taken and, because he was not their regular evening driver, she would not have recognised him.

It was a blessing that he had handed the grunt work over to his driver because he had just assumed that his wife would drive to wherever she wanted to go, or else take a taxi.

Anything but the tube and the bus.

He couldn't imagine that her father would ever have allowed her to hop on the number twenty-seven. Robert Bishop had excelled in being a snob.

He wondered whether this was all part of her sudden dislike of all things money and then he wondered how long the novelty of pretending not to care about life's little luxuries would last.

It was all well and good to talk about pious self-denial from the luxury of your eight-bedroomed mansion in the best postcode in London.

His lips curled derisively as he edged along through the traffic. She had been the apple of her father's eye and that certainly didn't go hand in hand with pious self-denial.

He cleared the traffic in central London, but found that he was still having to crawl through the stop-start tedium of traffic lights and pedestrian crossings, and it was after eleven by the time he pulled up in front of a disreputable building nestled amongst a parade of shops.

There was a betting shop, an Indian takeaway, a launderette, several other small shops and, tacked on towards the end of the row, a three-storeyed old building with a blue door. Dio was tempted to phone his driver and ask him whether he had texted the wrong address.

He didn't.

Instead, he got out of his car and spent a few moments

looking at the house in front of him. The paint on the door was peeling. The windows were all shut, despite the fact that it was another warm, sunny day.

His mind was finding it hard to co-operate. For once, he was having difficulty trying to draw conclusions from what his eyes were seeing.

He could hear the buzzing of the doorbell reverberating inside the house as he kept his hand pressed on the buzzer and then the sound of footsteps. The door opened a crack, chain still on.

'Dio!' Lucy blinked and wondered briefly if she might be hallucinating. Her husband had been on her mind so much as she had headed off but the physical reactions of her body told her that the man standing imperiously in front of her was no hallucination.

From behind her, Mark called out in his sing-song Welsh accent, 'Who's there, Lucy?'

'No one!' They were the first words that sprang into her head but, as her eyes tangled with Dio's, she recognised that she had said the wrong thing.

'No one...?' Dio's voice was soft, silky and lethally cool. The chain was still on the door and he laid his hand flat on it, just in case she got the crazy idea of trying to shut the door in his face.

'What are you doing here? You said that you were going to New York.'

'Who's the man, Lucy?'

'Did you follow me?'

'Just answer the question because, if you don't, I'll break the door down and find out myself.'

'You shouldn't be here! I… I…' She felt Mark behind her, inquisitively trying to peer through the narrow sliver to see who was standing at the door, and with a sigh of resignation she slowly slid the chain back with trembling fingers.

Dio congratulated himself on an impressive show of self-control as he walked into the hallway of the house which, in contrast to the outside, was brightly painted in shades of yellow. He clenched his fists at his sides, eyes sliding from Lucy to the man standing next to her.

'Who,' he asked in a dangerously low voice, 'the hell are you, and what are you doing with my wife?'

The man in front of him was at least three inches shorter and slightly built. Dio thought that he would be able to flatten him with a tap of his finger, and that was exactly what he wanted to do, but he'd be damned if he was going to start a brawl in a house.

Growing up on the wrong side of the tracks, however, had trained him well when it came to holding his own with his fists.

'Lucy, shall I leave you two to talk?'

'Dio, this is Mark.' She recognised the glitter of menace in her husband's eyes and decided that, yes, the best thing Mark could do would be to evaporate. Shame he wouldn't be able to take her with him, but perhaps the time had come to lay her cards on the table and tell Dio what was going on. Before he started punching poor Mark, who was fidgeting and glancing at her worriedly.

She felt sick as she looked, with dizzy compulsion, at the tight, angry lines of her husband's face.

'I'd shake your hand,' Dio rasped, 'but I might find myself giving in to the urge to rip it off, so I suggest you take my wife's advice and clear off, and don't return unless I give you permission.'

'Dio, please…' she pleaded, putting herself between

her husband and Mark. 'You've got the wrong end of the stick.'

'I could beat him to a pulp,' Dio remarked neutrally to her, 'without even bloodying my knuckles.'

'And you'd be proud of that, would you?'

'Maybe not proud, but eminently satisfied. So…' He pinned coldly furious silver eyes on the guy behind her. 'You clear off right now or climb out from your hiding place behind my wife and get what's coming to you!'

With a restraining hand on Dio's arm, Lucy turned to Mark and told him gently that she'd call him as soon as possible.

Dio fought the urge to deal with the situation in the most straightforward way known to mankind.

But what would be the point? He wasn't a thug, despite his background.

His head was cluttered with images of the fair-haired man, the fair-haired wimp who had hidden behind his wife, making love to Lucy.

The heat of the situation was such that it was only when the front door clicked shut behind the loser that Dio noticed what he should have noticed the very second he had looked at Lucy.

Gone were the expensive trappings: the jewellery, the watch he had given to her for her birthday present, the designer clothes…

He stared at her, utterly bemused. Her hair was scraped back into a ponytail and she was dressed in a white tee-shirt, a pair of faded jeans and trainers. She looked impossibly young and so damned sexy that his whole body jerked into instant response.

Lucy felt the shift in the atmosphere between them, although she couldn't work out at first where it was coming from. The tension was still there but threaded through that was a sizzling electrical charge that made her heart begin to beat faster.

'Are you going to listen to what I have to say?' She hugged her arms around her because she was certain that he would be able to see the hard tightening of her nipples against the tee-shirt.

'Are you going to spin me fairy stories?'

'I've never done that and I'm not going to start now.'

'I'll let that ride. Are you having an affair with that man?'

'No!'

Dio took a couple of steps towards her, sick to his stomach at the games going on in his head. 'You're my wife!'

Lucy's eyes shifted away from his. Her breathing was laboured and shallow and she was horrified to realise that, despite the icy, forbidding threat in his eyes, she was still horribly turned on. It seemed that something had been unlocked inside her and now she couldn't ram it back into a safe place, out of harm's way.

Dio held up his hand, as though interrupting a flow of conversation, although she hadn't uttered a word.

'And don't feed me garbage about being my wife in name only, because I sure as hell won't be buying it! You're my wife and I had better not find out that you've been fooling around behind my back!'

'What difference would it make?' she flung at him, her eyes simmering with heated rebellion. 'You fool around behind mine!'

'In what world do you think I'd fool around behind your back?' Dio roared, little caring what he said and not bothering to filter his words.

The silence stretched between them for an eternity. Lucy had heard what he had said but had she heard correctly? Had he really not slept with anyone in all the time they had been married? A wave of pure, undiluted relief washed over her and she acknowledged that resentment at her situation, at least in part, had been fuelled by the thought that he had been playing around with other women, having the sex she had denied him.

She would have liked to question him a bit more, tried to ascertain whether he was, indeed, telling the truth; if he was, more than anything else she would have loved to have ask him *why*.

'Now…' His thunderous voice crashed through her thoughts, catapulting her right back to the reality of him standing in front of her, having discovered the secret she had held to herself for the past couple of months. 'Who the hell was that man?'

'If you'd just stop shouting, Dio, I'll tell you everything.' Lucy eyed him warily.

'I'm waiting—and you'd better tell me something I want to hear.'

'Or else what?'

'You really don't want to know.'

'Oh, just stop acting like a Neanderthal and follow me…'

'Neanderthal? You haven't see me at my best!'

They stared at one another. Hell, she looked so damned hot! He should have obeyed his primitive instincts and laid down laws of ownership from the get-go. He should have had a bodyguard walk three inches behind her at all times. If he'd done that, he wouldn't be standing here now with his brain spiralling into freefall!

'Just come with me.' Lucy turned on her heels and

disappeared towards a room at the back, just beyond the staircase that led upwards, and he followed her.

'There!' She stepped aside and allowed him to brush past her, then looked at him as he, in turn, looked around him. Looked at the little desks, the low bookshelves crammed with books, the white board and the walls covered with posters.

'Not getting it,' Dio said, after he had turned full circle.

'It's a classroom!' Lucy controlled the desire to yell because he was just so pig-headed, just so consumed by the business of making money, that he couldn't think outside the box.

'Why are you seeing some man in a classroom?'

'I'm not *seeing some man in a classroom*!'

'Are you going to try and convince me that the loser I got rid of was a figment of my imagination?'

'Of course I'm not going to do that, Dio! Okay, so maybe I've been meeting Mark here over the past couple of months…'

'This has been going on for months?' He raked his fingers through his hair, but his blood pressure was at least getting back to normal, because she wasn't having an affair. He didn't know why he knew that but he did.

Which didn't mean that he wasn't interested in finding out just what *had* been going on…

'Oh, please, just sit down.'

'I'm all ears to hear what my wife's been getting up to when I've been out of the country.'

He dwarfed the chair and, even though he was now safely sitting down, he still seemed to emanate enough power to make her feel a bit giddy and unsteady on her feet.

'Did you plan this?' Lucy suddenly asked, arms still folded. 'I mean, when you told me that you were going to New York, did you lie, knowing that you intended to follow me?'

'A man has to do what a man has to do.' Dio shrugged, not bothering to deny the accusation. 'Although, if we're going to be completely accurate, *I* didn't follow you. Jackson, my driver, did. When he alerted me to your location, I drove here to find out what was going on.'

'That's as good as following me yourself!'

'It's better because I gather you took the tube and the bus to get here. It might have been difficult getting onto the same bus as you without you recognising me.'

'But why? Why now?'

'Why do you think, Lucy?'

'You never seemed to care one way or another what I got up to in your absences.'

'I never expected my wife to be running around with some man when I wasn't looking. I didn't think that I had to have you watched twenty-four-seven.'

'You don't. Didn't.' She flushed, recognising the measure of trust he had placed in her. She had met many women, wives of similarly wealthy men, whose every movement was monitored by bodyguards, who had little or no freedom. She had once mentioned that to Dio and he had dismissed that as the behaviour of paranoid, arrogant men who were so pumped up with their own self-importance that they figured the rest of the world wanted what they had.

It cut her to the quick now that he might think that his trust had been misplaced.

She hated him, she told herself stoutly, but she wasn't the sort of girl who would ever have fooled around.

Suddenly it seemed very, very important for her to make him believe that.

'I would never have done anything behind your back, Dio,' she said evenly. 'And I haven't. Mark and I are work mates.'

'Come again?'

'I follow a local website,' she told him. 'All sorts of things get posted. Advertisements for used furniture, rooms to let, book clubs looking for members. Mark posted a request for anyone interested in teaching maths to some of the underprivileged kids around here. I answered the ad.'

Dio stared at her, astounded at what he was hearing.

'I remember telling you once that I wanted to go into teaching.'

'I wanted to be a fireman when I was eight. The phase didn't last.'

'It's not the same thing!'

'Strange that you wanted to teach yet ended up marrying me and putting paid to your career helping the underprivileged.'

'I didn't think I had a choice!' Lucy answered hotly.

'We all have choices.'

'When it comes to…to…family, sometimes our choices are limited.'

Dio wryly read the subtext to that. There had been no way that she was going to leave Daddy to pay the price for his own stupidity and greed. Better that she put her own dreams and ambitions on hold. And of course, saving Daddy *had*, after all, come with a hefty financial sweetener…

'And, now your choices are wide open, you decided that you'd follow your heart's dream…'

'There's no need to be cynical, Dio. Don't *you* have any dreams you've ever wanted to follow?'

'Right now my imagination is working full-time on getting the honeymoon you failed to deliver…' And that was precisely how he intended to harness his roaming mind. He had fallen hard for what he had thought was her disingenuous innocence. If she thought that he was mug enough to repeat his mistake, by buying into the concept of the poor little rich wife whose only dream was to help the poor and the needy, then she was in for a surprise.

'You're not even interested in hearing about this place, are you?' she asked in a disappointed voice. 'When I told you that I wanted a divorce, you weren't even interested in asking me why.'

'Would you like me to ask you now?' Dio looked at her with raised eyebrows and Lucy drew in a couple of steadying breaths because he could be just so unbearable when he put his mind to it. He believed the worst of her and there was no way that he was going to revise his opinions, whatever she told him.

It didn't matter that *he* had married *her* for all the wrong reasons! He played by his own rules.

'Is all of this going to pay enough to keep the wolf from the door?' He spread his arms wide to encompass the little room but he kept his eyes fixed on her face. She looked as though she wanted to cry.

'It doesn't pay anything at all. It's all purely voluntary work.'

'Ah… And what's your relationship with the man who scarpered when I threatened to beat him up?'

'He didn't scarper.'

'Not the answer I want.'

'You're so arrogant, Dio!'

'I'm interested in finding out whether my wife has a crush on some man she met on the Internet!'

His voice was calm and only mildly curious but Lucy could sense the undercurrent of steel running through it. She shivered because, just for the briefest of seconds, she wondered what it would be like for that possessiveness in his voice to indicate jealousy.

She wondered what it would feel like to have this sinfully good-looking, charismatic and utterly arrogant man...*jealous*.

She shakily dismissed that insane curiosity before it even had time to take root.

'I don't have a crush on Mark,' she told him quietly. 'Although, he's just the sort of guy I might have a crush on.'

'What do you mean by that?' Dio was outraged that they were sitting here having this conversation.

'I mean he's a really nice guy. He's kind, he's considerate, he's thoughtful and the kids adore him.'

'Sounds like a barrel of laughs.'

'He can be,' Lucy retorted sharply. 'He can actually be very funny. He makes me laugh,' she added wistfully and Dio took a deep, steadying breath.

'And I don't?'

'We haven't laughed together since...'

Suddenly restless, he stood up and began pacing the room and, this time, he actually took in what he was seeing, all the evidence of classes in progress. He flicked through one of the exercise books lying on a desk and recognised his wife's handwriting. Ticks, corrections, encouraging smiley faces...

'So, no crush on the hapless teacher,' Dio eventually drawled. 'And is that reciprocated?'

For a moment, Lucy considered throwing caution to the winds and telling him that *the hapless teacher* was crazy about her. Something dark inside her wanted to see if she could make him jealous, even though she already knew that answer to that one.

'Mark isn't interested in women,' she said baldly. 'Not in that way. He's very happy with his partner who works for a legal firm in Kent. We're just good friends.'

Dio felt a bolt of pure satisfaction and he allowed himself to relax. It had been inconceivable that she had been fooling around behind his back. It was also inconceivable that he would allow her to walk away from him without him first sampling the body that had preyed on his mind ever since he had first laid eyes on her.

Whether she knew it or not, she was his weakness, and he was determined finally to put paid to that. The momentary threat of another man had shown him what he had casually assumed. He had allowed his pride to call the shots, to subdue a more primal instinct to assert himself under a civilised, remote veneer that just wasn't his style. No more. She was his and he wanted her, never more so than now, when she was stripped of the make-up and the designer clothes, when her raw beauty was on show. Her teacher friend might be gay but it still bothered Dio that the man had even seen her like this, in all her natural glory.

Her talk about some mythical man who was kind and caring, waiting out there for her, had also got on his nerves.

His eyes slid lazily to her face and he watched her for a few seconds in silence until he could see the tide of pink creep into her cheeks. When she began to fidget, he allowed his eyes to drift a little lower, slowly taking in the jeans, the tee-shirt and the jut of her pert little breasts underneath.

'So...' he murmured, finding a slightly more comfortable position. 'At least my woman hasn't been screwing around behind my back...'

'Since when am I *your woman*?'

'I like you like this.'

'What are you talking about?'

'Unadorned. It's sexy.'

Lucy went redder. She felt tell-tale moisture seep through her panties, felt an ache down there that throbbed and spread under the unhurried intensity of his gaze.

'I told you, I'm not interested...' But she could hear a wobble in her voice and the shadow of a smile that tugged his lips was telling. She straightened and gave herself a stern mental talking to. 'I'm going to build a life for myself, Dio. A real life—no pretending, no having to talk to people I don't want to talk to, no dressing up in clothes I don't like wearing!'

'Laudable.' He cocked his head to one side. 'So your plan is to continue your voluntary work here?'

'Like I said, it isn't all about money!'

'But you never qualified as a teacher, did you?'

'I will as soon as I can and the work I do here will be invaluable experience.'

'The place is falling down,' Dio pointed out. 'You might want to devote your talent for teaching here but, frankly, I doubt this building will stay the course. You may not have noticed, but there's a bad case of rising damp going on and I'd bet that the plumbing goes back to the Dark Ages.'

'Mark is doing an excellent job of trying to raise funds.'

'Really?'

Lucy didn't say anything for a while and Dio nodded slowly, reading what she was reluctant to tell him.

In hard times, it was always difficult to get well-meaning individuals to part with their cash and certainly, if they were providing a service to the needy, then the parents of those needy children would just not have the cash to give anyway.

The building was collapsing around them and neither of them would be able to stall the inevitable.

'I never knew you were so…engaged in wanting to do good for the community,' he murmured truthfully. 'And I'm willing to lend a hand here.'

'What are you talking about?' Lucy dragged her mind away from a brief picture of how her father would have reacted to what she was doing. With horror. He had always been an inveterate snob of the very worst kind. Women were not cut out for careers and certainly not careers that involved them dealing with people lower down the pecking order! A nice job working for a posh auction house might have met with his approval but teaching maths to school kids from a deprived background? Never in a month of Sundays.

To think of the kids not having this facility was heart breaking. She hadn't been there long, but she knew that Mark had poured his life and soul into trying to make something of the place. And the kids, a trickle which was steadily growing, would be the ones who fared worst.

'You want to walk away from our marriage with nothing rather than face getting into bed with me.' Dio didn't bother to gift wrap what he had to say and he didn't bother to point out that that kiss they had shared was proof positive that she wasn't immune to what he had to offer. 'I can't help that—but you want this building bought…? Repaired…? Turned into a functioning high-spec space…? No expense spared…? How does that sound to you, Lucy? You see…' He relaxed, met her bemused gaze coolly and steadily. 'I want you and I'm not above using any trick in the book to get what I want…'

CHAPTER FOUR

LUCY WAS APPALLED.

'What kind of thing is that for you to say?' she demanded shakily. 'You'd stoop so low?'

Dio inclined his beautiful head to one side and shrugged elegantly. 'I don't look at it that way.'

'No? And what way *do* you look at it?'

'I look at it as a form of persuasion.'

'I can't believe I'm hearing this.'

'You're my wife,' he said in the sort of voice that implied he was stating the glaringly obvious and irrefutable. 'When you started concocting your little plan to walk out of my life, you must surely have known that I wouldn't lie down on the ground waving a white flag and wishing you every success. Since when did I turn into that kind of person?'

Lucy shifted uncomfortably and then began fiddling with a pile of exercise books on the desk at which she had sat. Teacher in the front with wayward pupil facing her. Except Dio was far too intimidating to be any old wayward pupil.

'Well?' he prodded coolly.

'I just think it's out of order for you to jeopardise the

welfare of lots of deprived children who happen to be benefitting from what is on offer here!'

'I'm not jeopardising anyone's welfare. You are.' He glanced at his watch. He had been optimistic about getting back to the office at some point during the day and had thus dressed in his suit but, the way things were going, the office felt out of reach at the moment and, strangely enough, that didn't bother him.

He was far too invigorated by what was taking place.

'Is this taking longer than you expected?' Lucy asked with saccharin sweetness that wouldn't have fooled an idiot and he grinned.

Her stomach seemed to swoop and swirl inside her, as though she had been suddenly dropped from a great height without the aid of a parachute. That grin; it transformed the harsh, forbidding contours of his lean face. It reminded her of her youthful folly in letting it get under her skin until she had been walking on clouds, hanging onto his every word, waiting for the next meeting with barely bated breath.

And just like that it dawned on her why the thought of making love to him was so terrifying.

Yes, she hated him for the way he had manipulated her into marrying him for all the wrong reasons. Yes, she hated the way he had showcased her, like a business asset to be produced at will and then dispatched when no longer needed.

But what really scared her was the fact that he could still do things to her, make her feel things that were only appropriate in the domain of a real, functioning marriage.

When she thought of having him touch her, make love to her, she knew that somehow she would end up being vulnerable. He still got to her and she was scared stiff that, the closer he approached, the more ensnared she would become.

Like it or not, she was not nearly as detached as she had presented herself over time.

And that lazy grin was enough to remind her of that unwelcome reality.

'For my dear wife, I would be willing to put business on hold indefinitely.'

Lucy shot him a glance of scathing disbelief and Dio laughed, a rich, sexy, velvety sound that shot right past her defences.

'Or at least for a couple of hours, while we try to work out our little differences. Show me around.' He stood up and flexed his muscles. 'I can't carry on sitting in this chair for much longer. It's far too small. My joints are beginning to seize up. I need to stretch my legs, so give me the guided tour. If I'm going to revive this dump, I might as well start assessing what needs to be done.'

Lucy's full mouth compressed. Was he deliberately trying to goad a response out of her? Or was he just supremely confident of getting his own way, whatever she said to the contrary?

'You're not going to *revive this dump* and you're not interested in what I do here, anyway!'

Dio looked at her long and hard, hands thrust into his trouser pockets.

'I'm going to disagree on both counts,' he told her softly.

Lucy's eyes fluttered and she looked away hurriedly. The dark, naked intent in his gaze was unsettling. She decided that showing him around the school, what little there was of it, was a better option than standing here and having to brave the full frontal force of his personality.

She gave a jerky shrug and directed him to the exercise books on her desk. This was the main classroom, where she and Mark did their best to accommodate the children, whose abilities varied wildly, as did their ages.

She warmed to her subject.

Dio saw what had been missing all these months. She had presented a beautiful, well-educated, cultured mask to the outside world but the animation had gone. It was here now as she talked about all the wonderful things the school was capable of providing; how much the considerate, funny and thoughtful Mark had managed to do with minimum help and almost no funding. Her eyes glowed and her cheeks pinked. She gestured and he found himself riveted by the fluid grace of her hands as she spoke.

There were several rooms on the ground floor. The building was like the Tardis, much bigger inside than it appeared from the outside.

'Volunteer teachers come whenever they can,' she told him, leading the way into another small room. 'Mark has managed to get a rota going and several subjects are now covered by experts.' She looked at Dio and her voice softened. 'You wouldn't believe the conditions some of the kids who come to us live in,' she explained. 'The fact that they're brought to us in the first place shows a great deal of parental support but there are stories of almost no food, noise pollution from neighbours, overcrowding in small flats…the list goes on.'

Dio nodded and let his eyes drift over that full mouth, the slim column of her neck, her narrow shoulders. Vanilla-blonde strands of hair were escaping the confines of the ponytail and the way they wisped around her face made her look incredibly young, barely a teenager.

'How safe is it?' he asked suddenly.

'Huh?'

'What are the safety procedures around here? Is there just the pair of you working here? And have you been working at night?'

'Are you telling me that you're concerned for my welfare?' Lucy's voice was mocking.

'Always.'

She felt the steady thud of her heart banging against her rib cage. His face was so serious that she was momentarily deprived of the power of speech and, when she did rediscover her vocal cords, she could hear a thread of jumpiness in her voice as she explained that neither of them worked nights and the place was always busy with people coming and going during the handful of hours in which they did work.

'Be that as it may,' Dio continued, 'now that I know where you spend your time, and what you get up to when I'm not around, you're going to have two of my guards close at hand whenever you come here—and, Lucy, that's not negotiable.'

'You used to say that you didn't agree with men who felt that they had to surround their wives with bodyguards!'

'You wouldn't require a bodyguard if you spent your time doing your nails and shopping...which was what I thought you got up to in your spare time.'

'What sort of impression is that going to give?' Lucy cried, feeling the wings of her freedom being clipped and resenting it even as she warmed with forbidden pleasure at the thought of him wanting to protect her.

To protect his investment. She brought herself back down to earth with a sobering bump. An investment he was keen to look after now that he wanted to take full advantage of it before he consigned it to the rubbish bin.

'I've never cared about what other people think. So, how many classrooms are there in this place and what's upstairs…?'

'I can't have great big, bulky men lurking around. They'll scare off the kids.'

'I doubt that in this neighbourhood.'

'Stop being provocative, Dio!'

'If you think I'm being provocative, then how would you describe yourself?' He strolled towards her and she found herself nailed to the spot, mesmerised by the casual grace of his movements.

'I'm just…just trying to tell you that I don't want to…to…stand out when I come here.' Perspiration beaded her upper lips as he curled a strand of wayward hair around his finger. 'What are you doing, Dio?'

'I'm talking to you. You can't object if your soon-to-be ex-husband takes a little interest in the safety and well-being of his wife, can you?'

'That's not what I meant.'

'No?' He looked perplexed. 'Then what did you mean?'

'You… I…' Her sluggish brain could not complete the remainder of her thoughts. Her body felt heavy and lethargic. Right now, she yearned for him to touch her in other places; she absolutely yearned for him to take her to all those places he frequently took her to in her dreams.

She had to exert every ounce of willpower to drag herself physically out of his mesmerising radius, stepping back and sucking in a lungful of restorative air.

'It won't work having great big guys standing on either side of me. Plus, when I come here, no one knows who I am.'

'You're not recognised?' Dio frowned and she allowed herself a little smile.

'Why would anyone recognise me? I dress like this, in jeans, tee-shirts and jumpers, and I scrape my hair back and I don't wear tons of make-up and expensive jewellery.'

He heard the derision in her voice and was struck, once again, at hidden depths swirling just out of sight.

It confused him and that was a sensation he was not accustomed to dealing with. Least of all in a woman whose motivations had left him in no doubt as to the sort of person she was. Not one with hidden depths, for starters.

He raked his fingers through his hair and shook his head impatiently, clearing it of the sudden fog of doubt that had descended.

Did she enjoy the novelty of pretending to do good undercover? Was that it?

'Now, you were asking about the other rooms downstairs.' She briskly took him on the tour he had requested. More rooms with more low bookshelves and a scattering of stationery. She could have equipped the entire school with computers had she so desired simply by flogging one of the items of jewellery locked away in the safe in her bedroom. But she had chosen not to and he presumed that that was because she wanted, as she had told him, to keep her identity under wraps. To keep the extent of her wealth under wraps.

And yet how did that make sense?

She had been a Bishop, through and through. Surely the last thing she should have wanted would be...*this*.

He looked around at the shabby walls which someone had optimistically painted a cheerful yellow, similar to the walls in the hallway. Nothing could conceal the wear and tear of the fabric of the building, however, and the fact that it was practically falling down.

'Mark should be back shortly.' She ended the down-stairs tour in a room that was very similar to the others he had been shown. 'If you're really interested, you can ask him whatever questions you like.'

'Think I'll pass on that one.' He leaned against the wall and looked at his wife whose face had become smudged with pencil at some point during their tour. 'I wouldn't want to have to administer smelling salts because he has a fainting fit seeing me still here.'

'Very funny,' Lucy muttered, making sure to keep a healthy distance.

'I have some questions to ask *you*, though. Is there anywhere around here we can go for lunch?'

'Lunch?' she parroted, because lunch, just the two of them, was not something they had done since getting married.

'Unless you've travelled with sandwiches and a flask of hot coffee…? In your anxious attempts not to stand out…?' He could have told her that she stood out just looking the way she did.

'There's a café just round the corner.'

'Café?'

'It's not much but they make nice enough sandwiches and serve very big mugs of tea.'

'I'll give that one a miss. Any other suggestions?'

Lucy eyed him coolly and folded her arms. 'You're in my territory now, Dio.'

'*Your* territory? Don't make me laugh.'

'I don't care what you think but I feel I belong here a lot more than I belong in any of those soulless big houses, where I've had to make sure the fridges are stocked with champagne and caviar and the curtains are cleaned on a regular basis just in case…'

Dio's lips thinned. 'If you're trying to annoy me, then congratulations, Lucy—you're going about it the right way.'

'I'm not trying to annoy you but I meant what I said. If you want to continue this conversation and ask whatever questions you want to ask, including questions about the divorce I've asked you for, then you can jolly well eat in the café Mark and I eat in whenever we're here! I can't believe you're such a snob.'

'I'm not a snob,' Dio heard himself reply in an even, well-measured voice. 'But maybe I've seen enough of those greasy spoon cafés to last a lifetime. Maybe I come from enough of a deprived background to know that getting out of it was the best thing I ever did. I certainly have no desire to pretend that it holds any charm for me now.'

Lucy's mouth fell open.

This was the first time Dio had ever mentioned his background. She had known, of course, that he had made his own way up in the world, thanks to her father's passing, derogatory remarks. But to hear him say anything, anything at all, was astounding.

Dio flushed darkly and turned away. 'I'll talk to you when you return home this evening.'

'No!' Seeing him begin walking towards the door galvanised Lucy into action and she placed a detaining hand on his arm.

Just like that, heat from his body seared through her,

and she almost yanked her hand back as if it had been physically burnt.

'We...we should talk now,' she stammered, stepping back. 'I know you must have been shocked at what I've asked and I never thought that you would...well, that you would see what I've been up to here...but, now that you have, well, I don't mind having lunch with you somewhere a little smarter.'

Dio sighed and shook his head before fixing fabulous, silver eyes on her flushed face. 'Take me to the café. It's no big deal.'

She locked up behind her and they walked side by side to the café where she and Mark were regulars.

She was desperate to ask him about his past. Suddenly it was as though locked doors had been opened and curiosity was bursting out of her.

He'd grown up without money but had he been happy? As she knew only too well from personal experience, a moneyed background was no guarantee of happiness.

She sneaked a glance at his averted profile and concluded that he wasn't in the mood for a soul-searching chit chat on his childhood experiences.

And it surprised her that she was so keen to hear all about them.

'It's not much,' she reminded him as they pulled up in front of a café that was still relatively empty and smelled heavily of fried food.

'Understatement of the year.' Dio looked down at her and noticed the way the sun glinted off her blonde hair; noticed the thick lushness of her lashes and the earthy promise of her full lips. His breathing became a little shallower. 'But I won't forget the virtues of the brimming cups of tea and the big sandwiches...'

They knew her!

Dio was stunned. Two of the people working behind the counter had kids who had started drifting in to do maths lessons and there was a brief chat about progress.

'And this…' she turned to Dio and glanced away quickly '…is a friend. Someone thinking of investing in the building, really turning it into somewhere smarter and better equipped…' She felt him bristle next to her. She'd always removed her wedding ring before coming here; it was just too priceless to take chances. She sneaked a sideways glance and caught the look of annoyance in his eyes and she returned that look of simmering annoyance with a special look of her own, one that was earnest and serious. 'He's very interested in helping the kids in this area really reach their full potential at school.'

'Because…' Dio said instantly, with the sort of charming smile that would knock anyone off balance, which it seemed to be doing to Anita, whose mouth had dropped open the second she had clocked him. 'Because I happen to have grown up not a million miles from here,' he said smoothly. 'On an estate not unlike the one we passed and, take it from me, the only way to escape is through education.'

Anita was nodding vigorously. John was agreeing in a manly fashion. Lucy was feeling as though she had been cleverly outmanoeuvred.

'This lovely young woman and I…are in discussions at the moment. It could all hinge on her acceptance of my proposal: no more rising damp, all the rooms brought up to the highest specification. Naturally, I would buy the building outright, and the cherry on the cake would be the equipment I would install. I find that computers are part and parcel of life nowadays. How else can children access vital information? Like I said, though, Lucy and I are in talks at the moment…'

As soon as they were seated, with mugs of steaming tea and two extra-large doorstop sandwiches filled to bursting in front of them, Lucy leaned forward, glaring.

'Thanks for that, Dio!'

'Any time. What else are friends and potential investors for? Why didn't you introduce me as your husband?'

'Because there would have been loads of questions to field,' Lucy said defensively. 'They would want to know who I really was…'

'To have snagged me?'

'You have a ridiculous ego.' She sipped some tea and looked at him over the rim of the mug. 'Were you lying when you said what you said?'

Dio knew exactly what she was talking about. Why had he suddenly imparted information about his past? He had always kept the details of his background to himself. Growing up on a tough estate, where the laws of the jungle were very different from the jungle laws of the business world, he had learnt the wisdom of silence. It was a habit that was deeply ingrained.

'Be more specific,' he drawled. 'Nice sandwich, by the way.'

'Did you grow up near here?'

'We *are* breaking into new and unexplored territory, aren't we?' he murmured, his fabulous eyes roving over the stunning prettiness of her heart-shaped face. It amazed him that he had never seen that body. His success with women had started at a very young age and was legendary and yet, with her, *his wife*, he had yet to discover what lay underneath the tee-shirt and the jeans.

Bitterness refused to dampen the sudden thrust of his

erection and it occurred to him that he had spent an awful lot of time fantasising about the untouchable ice-maiden who had conned him into marriage.

Not for much longer. That was a very satisfying thought.

'Unexpected announcements, revelations all round, time together without high society peering over our shoulders… Where does it end, I wonder? Oh, yes, I know. In bed.'

Lucy flushed. Those amazing pale eyes sent her nervous system into freefall and as soon as he mentioned the word 'bed' she couldn't stop the tide of graphic images that pelted into her head at breakneck speed.

The principles she had held so dear became gossamer-thin under the impact of those images.

But for her, sex and love were entwined. They were!

'You were out of order implying to John and Anita that you were willing to sink money in the place if I agreed to your demands.'

'Was I?' Dio shot her a perplexed frown. 'I thought that I was only being honest. Nice people, by the way. They seem to have bought into the usefulness of having the after-school tutoring scheme there, but then I guess they would, considering they both have children who attend. Must be tough.'

Lucy was beginning to feel as though she had been stuck in a washing machine with the speed turned to full.

'What must be tough?' She knew what was tough. Tough was the way her carefully laid plans had unravelled at the speed of light in the space of twenty-four short hours. She had suspected that talk of divorce wouldn't fall on completely fertile ground, because her husband was nothing if not proud, but she had not banked on the route he had taken which had now landed them both up here.

With talk of sex shimmering between them.

'Tough being a working parent, trying to make ends meet while still attempting to find the spare time to sit and do homework with kids. I guess that's the situation with your two...friends.'

'They're going to repeat what you told them to Mark.'

'Oh dear. And would that be a problem?'

'You always have to get your own way, don't you?' Lucy looked at him resentfully and then immediately diverted her eyes, because he was just too sexy and too good-looking to stare at for very long. Especially now that the dynamics between them had changed, subtly but dramatically.

'Always,' Dio confirmed readily. 'What do you think your caring, sharing friend will think when he discovers that you're the person standing between the success and failure of his little baby...? Because, from what you've told me, this has been more than just a flash in the pan, try-it-on-for-size experiment for him.'

Lucy bristled. 'Are you implying that that's what it's been for me?' she demanded, sinking her teeth into her sandwich and chewing angrily on it.

'I never noticed just how cute you are when you're angry,' Dio murmured. 'But then, anger didn't score high on the list of required emotions in our marriage, did it?'

It surprised him just how much he was enjoying himself. Was it the bizarre novelty of the situation? He didn't know and he wasn't going to waste time with pointless questions. He was in very little doubt that as soon as he had had her, as soon as he had slept with her, he would regain healthy perspective on just the kind of woman she was, at which point he would bid farewell to his manipulative wife. But in the meantime…

Lucy lowered her eyes, reminded of just how hollow and empty their marriage had been, and then further reminded of all the high hopes and girlish dreams that had driven her to marry him in the first place.

'I find working with these kids fulfilling,' she told him, ignoring his barb. 'Much, much more fulfilling than making stupid small talk to people I don't like and barely know. Much more fulfilling than going to the opening of an art gallery or a society wedding.'

Privately, Dio couldn't have agreed more. One of the more odious things he had to do in his steady, inexorable rise to the very top of the pecking order was attend events he couldn't give a damn about. But it came with the job and he was too much of a realist to think otherwise.

Funnily enough, it had never occurred to him that his well-bred wife would ever have found that side of life a bore. In fact, he would have thought that that might have been one of the many things she enjoyed about the position into which she had cleverly manoeuvred herself.

Now he looked at her with a frown, trying to work out the little inconsistencies he was beginning to spot underneath the polished veneer he had always associated with her.

'It's going to be all round the neighbourhood that a big shot investor has taken an interest in our little local after-school club.'

'Not just any old big shot investor, though.'

'What am I supposed to say?' she demanded, pushing her plate to one side, making sure to keep her voice low and calm because people were beginning to filter into the café now and curious looks were being directed at them.

'You could tell them that you didn't care for the terms your big shot investor demanded.'

'You should never have followed me!'

'You know you want me…'

'I beg your pardon!'

'Shocking, isn't it?' He leant back in the chair and was amused when she leaned forward, all the better to make sure that their conversation wasn't overheard. 'You don't want to face up to it, but let's cut to the chase. You're hot for me.'

'I am not!'

'Would you like to put that to the test?' He cast his eyes round the small café and the curious faces. 'Why doesn't the hot shot investor apply a little physical pressure…? Hmm…? How about I reach across this table and kiss you? Remember that kiss? How about we have a repeat performance right here? Right now? Then we could take a vote…find out how many people agree with me that you're attracted to me…'

'You took me by surprise when you kissed me!' Patches of red had appeared on her cheeks. She knew that she didn't look like the calm, composed teacher everyone around here expected her to be. She looked just like she felt. Hassled, overwhelmed, confused.

Excited…

'So this time you'll be prepared. We can both gauge just how much you can withstand what's simmering between us.'

'There's nothing simmering between us!' Desperation threaded her voice.

'Of course there is.' Dio dismissed her in a hard, inflexible voice. 'And it's been there all the way through our sexless marriage.'

'Shh!'

He ignored her frantic interruption. 'I've seen the way you've looked at me when you thought you weren't being observed. You may have connived your way into marriage, and then pulled back once you'd got me hooked, but you still can't quite help what you feel, can you?'

Lucy rested her head in her hand and wondered if she could just wish herself some place else.

'Tell me...did you find it offensive to think of me in terms of being your lover?'

She looked at him, horrified. 'How can you say that? What are you talking about?'

'We couldn't have come from more opposite sides of the tracks,' Dio said drily. 'Did you imagine you might catch a working class infection if you got too close to me?'

'I'm not like that! We didn't have a proper marriage and I wasn't going to...to...'

He waved aside her half-baked, stammering explanation with an air of sudden boredom. 'Not really interested in going down this road,' he drawled. 'The only thing I want is *you*, my beloved wife. I want to feel your naked body writhing under me. I want to hear you scream out my name and beg me to bring you to orgasm.'

'That'll never happen!'

'Oh, it will. You just need to give the whole thing a little bit of thought and stop pretending that it'll be any great hardship for you. It won't be.'

'And you know this because...?' She was aiming for snappy and sarcastic; she got reedy and plaintive.

'Because I know women. Trust me. It won't be a hardship. And just think of the rewards... Fat alimony allowance...your little school shiny and well-equipped...grateful parents and happy little children… Could there be a better start to your wonderful bid for freedom…?' He leaned forward so that they were both now resting their elbows on the table, their faces close together, locked in their own private world. 'In fact, I have a splendid idea. Let's take our honeymoon, Lucy. Two weeks. After that, I have to be in Hong Kong to close a deal on a company buyout. I'll head there and you can… Well, you can begin your life of independence. How does that sound…?'

CHAPTER FIVE

PREY TO WARRING EMOTIONS, Lucy was left to consider her options for three days while Dio disappeared to Paris for an emergency meeting with the directors of one of his companies over there.

By her calculation, that left eleven days of honeymoon time before he vanished across the Atlantic to Hong Kong.

She knew that she had been cleverly but subtly outmanoeuvred.

For a start, the story of the brand new school spread like a raging wild fire. He had played the 'hot shot investor' to perfection. Now, as far as everyone in the neighbourhood was concerned, ordering computers, stationery and getting the builders in was just a little formality because everything was signed, sealed and delivered bar the shouting.

If the whole pipe dream collapsed, Lucy knew that she would have to dig deep to find an excuse that would work. The blame would fall squarely on her shoulders.

The day after she and Dio had lunched in the café, Mark had arrived at work clutching brochures for computers and printers. He had made noises about getting the national press involved to cover a 'feel good' story because 'the world was a dark place and it was just so damn heart-warming to find that there were still one or two heroes left in it'…

Lucy had nearly died on the spot. In what world could Dio Ruiz be classed as a hero?

No one had actually asked what the mysterious conditions were that had been imposed on her, for which she was very grateful, because she had no idea what she would have said.

They had been dependent on various money-raising ventures and government help to cover the scant lease on the building; now two members of the local council descended, beaming, to tell her that there were plans afoot to buy the place outright. They delivered a rousing speech on how much it would benefit the community to have the place brought up to scratch and in permanent active use.

They dangled the carrot of helping to subsidise three full-time members of staff who could perhaps assist in teaching non-English-speaking students, of which there were countless in the borough.

And, twice daily, Dio had called her on her mobile, ostensibly to find out how she was—given their new relationship, which involved conversation—but really, she knew, to apply pressure.

Two weeks…

And then, after that, freedom was hers for the taking.

Was he right? Would sleeping with him be such a hardship? They were married and, when she had married him, she had been hot for him, had counted the hours, the minutes and the seconds till they could climb into bed together. Her virginity was something precious to be handed over to him and she hadn't been able to wait to do it.

She was still a virgin but she was now considerably more cynical than she had once been. And how precious was it, really? So once upon a time she had had a dream of only marrying for love and losing her virginity to a guy she wanted to spend her life with. She had woken up. Big deal.

And she was *still* hot for him. It pained her to admit it, especially since he had gloatingly pointed it out to her and, worse, had proved it by kissing her, feeling her melt under his hands.

What was the point in denying reality? She'd been damned good at facing reality so far; she had not once shied away from the fact that she was trapped in a marriage and forced to play the part of the socialite she probably should have but never had been.

On day three she picked up her mobile to hear his dark, velvety voice down the line and, as usual, she felt the slow, thick stir of her heightened senses.

Once more or less able to withstand the drugging effect of his personality, Lucy had now discovered that her defences had been penetrated on all fronts. Even when he was on the opposite side of the world, she just had to hear his voice and every nerve inside her body quivered in response.

Overnight it seemed as though all the walls she had painstakingly built between them had been knocked down in a single stroke.

'What are you up to?'

Lucy sat down. Was she really interested in launching into a conversation about the porridge she had just eaten?

'Marie has handed in her notice. I knew she was going to at some point. She's far too ambitious to be cleaning. She's got a placement at a college. So I'm afraid you're going to have to find someone else to do the cleaning in the Paris apartment.'

'*I'm* going to have to find someone else?'

'Well, I won't be around, will I?' Lucy pointed out bluntly. She projected to when she would shut the door of their grand, three-storey mansion in London for good and she felt her heart squeeze inside her.

Sitting in the first class lounge at JFK airport, Dio frowned. By the time he returned to London, he wanted an answer from her, and the only answer he was prepared to accept was the one he wanted to hear.

That was what he wanted to chat about now. He certainly didn't want to have a tedious conversation about their apartment in Paris and finding a cleaner to replace the one who had quit. He didn't want her to start the process of withdrawing from the marriage. No way. Nor had he contemplated the prospect of not getting what he wanted from her.

It occurred to him that there really was only one topic of conversation he was willing to hear.

'I'll cross the bridge of hiring a new cleaner when the time comes.'

'Well, it'll come in the space of two weeks, which is when Marie will be leaving.'

'What are you wearing? It's early over there...are you still in your pyjamas? Does it strike you as a little bizarre that we've never seen each other in the confines of a bedroom, wearing pyjamas?'

Lucy went bright red and cleared her throat. 'I don't know what my clothes have to do with anything...' She automatically pulled her dressing gown tighter around her slender body and was suddenly conscious of her braless breasts and the skimpiness of her underwear.

'I'm making small talk. If we're to spend the next two weeks together—'

'Eleven days,' Lucy interrupted.

Dio relaxed and half-smiled to himself. He had made sure to phone her regularly while he had been away. Over the marriage, they had managed to establish a relationship in which she had been allowed to retreat. That retreat was not going to continue.

And now, without her having to say it, he could hear the capitulation in her voice. It generated the kick of an intense, slow burn of excitement.

'If we're to spend the next eleven days together, then we need to be able to converse.'

'We know how to converse, Dio. We've done a great deal of that over the course of our marriage.'

'Superficial conversation,' Dio inserted smoothly. 'No longer appropriate, given the fact that our relationship has changed.'

'Our relationship hasn't changed.'

'No? I could swear you just told me how long we're going to be spending on our long-overdue honeymoon...'

Lucy licked her lips nervously. The dressing gown had slipped open and, looking down, she could see the smooth lines of her stomach and her pert, pointed breasts.

She had made her mind up about his ultimatum and she hadn't even really been aware of doing so.

Soon that flat stomach and those breasts would be laid bare for him to see and touch.

A little shiver raced through her. She slipped her finger beneath her lacy briefs and felt her own wetness. It shocked her. It was as if her body was already reacting to the knowledge that someone else would be touching it—that *Dio* would be touching it.

'Okay,' she said as loftily as she could manage. 'So, you win, Dio. I hope it makes you feel proud.'

'Right now, pride is the very least of the things I'm feeling.' His voice lowered, sending a ripple of forbidden excitement through her.

Out of all the reasons she had privately given herself for yielding to his demands, she now acknowledged the only reason that really truly counted for anything.

It had nothing to do with the school, duty towards her students or, least of all, money.

She had yielded because she fancied him and because she knew, as he did, that to walk away from a dry marriage would be to wonder for ever what it might have been like to sleep with him.

Her head might not want to get into bed with Dio but her body certainly did and this was her window.

The fact that there were a lot of up sides and bonuses attached to her decision was just an added incentive.

'I'd tell you what I'm feeling,' he said roughly, 'but I'm sitting in the lounge at JFK and I wouldn't want anyone to start noticing the hefty bulge in my trousers…'

'Dio! That's…that's…'

'I know. Unfortunate, considering I'm going to have to wait a few more hours before I can be satisfied.'

'That's not what I meant!'

'No?'

'No,' Lucy told him firmly. To add emphasis to her denial, she very firmly tightened the dressing gown so that she could cover up her treacherously over-heated, semi-naked body. 'I… I'm happy to discuss the details of…er…our arrangement.'

'Speak English,' Dio said drily.

'I'll do this honeymoon business with you but only because I don't have a choice.'

'That's not very enthusiastic,' Dio admonished, hanging onto his temper. If he could put his feelings to one side, if he could forget her duplicitous take on their marriage, then he was damned if he was going to let her get away with dragging her feet and somehow blaming him for the fact that she wanted to sleep with him.

'Everyone expects you to descend and start flinging money at the school.'

'I find it doesn't do to mould your life according to other people's expectations.'

'How do I know that once this so-called honeymoon of ours is over you'll do what you say…?'

'You don't.' Dio was affronted. He had always been a man of his word, which was saying something, in a world where very few men were. He might not have been born with a silver spoon in his mouth but he knew one thing for sure: in his business practices, and in fact in his whole approach to life, he was a damned sight more ethical than a lot of his counterparts whose climb up the ladder had been a great deal less precarious than his had been!

'You'll have to rely on that little thing called trust.'

Lucy didn't say anything and Dio felt the significance of her silence like a disapproving slap on the face.

Rich, coming from the ice-maiden who had strung him along.

'I'm not a man who breaks his word,' he said coolly. 'I know many who do.'

Lucy thought of her father, who had cheated so many people out of their pensions, and she flushed guiltily. Were Dio's thoughts running along the same lines? He might have married her for all the wrong reasons but then he had never claimed to love her, had he? Even when they had been dating, he had never talked about love.

And something deep inside her knew that, if he had given his word, then he wasn't going to break it.

'Shall I book somewhere?' she asked stiffly. 'I expect you want to use one of the houses…'

'I think you can climb out of "personal assistant" mode on this occasion,' Dio said softly. 'It somehow ruins the…sizzle.'

His husky voice was doing all sorts of peculiar things to her body and she squirmed on the chair, idly glancing round at all the top-notch, expensive equipment in the very expensive kitchen.

'I surely need to book flights for us?' Lucy intended to do her very best not to let either of them forget that their weird honeymoon was built on stuff that was very prosaic.

This wasn't going to be one of those romantic affairs where they would spend their time whispering sweet nothings and staring longingly at one another over candlelit dinners before racing to their room so that they could rip the clothes off one another.

This was more getting something elemental out of their systems.

'Don't give it a thought,' Dio said briskly. 'I'll get my secretary to do the necessary.'

'But where will we be going? And when, exactly?'

'I'm at JFK now. When I return to London, I'll have a quick turnaround. Be prepared to be out of the country this time tomorrow.'

'What? I can't just leave here at a moment's notice.'

'Of course you can. My secretary will take care of everything. You just need to get ready for me...'

'Get ready for you?'

Dio laughed at the outrage in her voice. He was so hard for her right now, he was finding it difficult to move.

Small, high breasts... He had glimpsed the shadow of her cleavage in some of the more daring dresses she had worn to social events over the course of the marriage. He wondered what colour her nipples were. She was a natural blonde and he imagined that they were rosy pink, kissable nipples. He wondered what she would taste like when he buried himself between her thighs.

He wondered who else she had shared her body with before she had met him.

It was a grimly unappealing thought and he ditched it before it had time to take root.

'Use your imagination,' he drawled. 'Get into the head set...'

'Yes, sir...' Lucy muttered under her breath and she heard his soft laughter down the end of the line. Sexy laughter. The laughter of a man who'd got exactly what he wanted. She fidgeted a little more and forced herself to focus. 'And what should I pack?'

'Don't. I'll make sure that there are clothes waiting for you at the other end.'

'I don't want to be dressed up like a Barbie doll,' she told him quickly. 'That's not part of this arrangement.'

'I shall see you very soon, Lucy...'

'But you still haven't told me where we'll be going!'

'I know. Isn't it exciting? I, for one, can't wait.'

And he disconnected. Lucy was left holding a dead

phone and feeling panicked because now there was no going back.

She tried to think of life after the next ten days but she found her mind getting stuck with images of Dio in bed with her. After she had discovered the truth behind their sham of a marriage, she had told herself that that was why he had not tried to get her into bed before they had tied the knot.

She had thought that he was being a gentleman, respecting her wish to wait until they were married before having sex. She had been too embarrassed to tell him that she was still a virgin, and anyway the subject had not arisen.

Instead, he had been stringing her along. She had stopped day dreaming about him but the day dreams were rearing their heads once again and she couldn't stop them.

How was she supposed to travel to some unknown destination? They could be going to the Arctic, the Caribbean or a city somewhere. Had he even decided or was he going to let his assistant choose where they went?

And what was it going to be like when he returned to the house?

The knowledge that they would be cooped up together for the better part of a fortnight would lie between them like a lead weight…

Wouldn't it?

She was a bundle of nerves as evening drew round. For the first time in as long as she could remember, she didn't dress up for his arrival. Usually, she never dropped the role unless she was on her own. Usually he saw her formally attired, even when she was in casual clothing.

But things were different and she had defiantly chosen

to wear a pair of jeans and a faded old tee-shirt from her university days. Nor was she plastered with make-up and she hadn't curled her hair. Instead, she was a make-up-free zone and her hair hung heavily just past her shoulders, neatly tucked behind her ears.

She was in the same place as she had been when she had confronted him with talk of divorce, standing in the drawing room. And she was just as jumpy.

And yet, staring through the window into the, for London, relatively large garden with its row of perfectly shaped and manicured shrubs, she didn't hear him until he spoke.

'I wondered if you would wait up for me.' Dio strolled into the drawing room, dumping his jacket, which he had hooked over his shoulder. It had been a tiresome flight, even in first class, but he felt bright eyed and bushy-tailed now as he flicked his eyes over her.

He'd half-expected her to go into a self-righteous meltdown between speaking to her on the phone and showing up at the house. She was very good at adopting the role of blameless victim. He guessed that the lure of money was irresistible, however. She might play at her volunteer work and make big plans to teach but teaching didn't pay nearly enough for her to afford the sort of lifestyle to which she had always been accustomed.

Cynicism curled his lips when he thought that.

'Drink?'

A feeling of déjà vu swept over Lucy as she helplessly followed him into the kitchen, although this time she had eaten, and she expected he would have as well, so there would be no pretend domesticity preparing a meal.

'I thought we could chat about plans for tomorrow,' she began valiantly. 'I need to know what time we will be leaving. I… I've packed a couple of things…' He looked drop-dead gorgeous and she could feel the electricity in the air between them, sparking like a live, exposed wire. It made the hairs on the back of her neck stand on end.

And the way he was looking at her, his pale eyes skewering her, brought her out in a nervous wash of perspiration.

She wanted crisply to remind him that their arrangement was for the honeymoon period, which technically would only start when they reached wherever they were heading, and so for tonight they would retreat to their separate quarters as per normal. However, her tongue seemed to have become glued to the roof of her mouth.

'Have you been thinking about me?' Dio asked lazily. 'Because I've been thinking about you.' And marvelling that it had taken them this long to get where they were now, but then again the whole question of the penniless divorce had driven the situation.

He walked slowly towards her and she gave a little nervous squeak. 'I thought we were going to…er…well, when we were away…'

'Why stand on ceremony? The honeymoon's been cut a little short by my unexpected meeting in New York anyway, so fair's fair, wouldn't you say? I don't want to be short-changed on time. If I'm to pay for two weeks, then I want my two weeks, or as good as…'

The last thing Lucy was expecting was to be swept off her feet. Literally. The breath whooshed out of her body as she was carried out of the kitchen. She felt the thud as he nudged the door open with his foot and then she was bouncing against him, heart racing as he took her up the stairs.

To his bedroom, which she had been into many times

before. It was a marvel of masculinity. The colours were deep and rich, the furniture bold and dark with clean lines. Even with her eyes squeezed tightly shut, she could visualise it. Once, when he had gone away, leaving the house a lot earlier to catch a transatlantic flight, she had gone into the bedroom to air it before the cleaner came and had remained frozen to the spot at the sight of the rumpled bed, still bearing the impression of where he had been lying. She could remember tentatively touching it and then springing back because it had still held the lingering warmth of his body.

It had shaken her more than she had thought possible.

He dumped her on the bed and then stood back, arms folded, for once lost as to what his next move might be.

He had been fired up with confidence downstairs, when he had hoisted her into his arms like a true caveman and brought her to his bedroom. But now…

She looked unimaginably beautiful and unimaginably fragile, her eyes wide and apprehensive, making him feel like a great, hulking thief who had snatched her from her bed and carried her off to his cave so that he could have his wicked way.

Dio raked his fingers through his hair and moved to the window where he stood for a few seconds, looking outside, before snapping the wooden shutters closed, blocking out the street light.

Lucy stared at him from under her lashes. Her heart was still pounding and the blood was still rushing through her veins, hot and fierce. She wanted him so badly right now that she felt like she might die of longing, yet he was just standing there, looking at her with brooding stillness.

Maybe he had come to his senses, she thought.

Maybe he had realised that you couldn't just bargain with someone's fate the way he had with hers. Maybe he had seen the light and come to the conclusion that to blackmail someone into sleeping with you just wasn't on.

And if that was the case then why wasn't she feeling happier? Why wasn't she sitting up and making a case for having her divorce without a bunch of stupid stipulations? Why wasn't she striking while the iron was hot, trying to locate Mr Decent who must surely be there hiding behind Mr Caveman?

She wasn't feeling happier because she wanted him, simple as that.

Maybe if he had never mentioned sleeping with her, had never looked at her with those amazing, lazy, sexy eyes, she would have walked away from their marriage with her head held high and all her principles burning a hole inside her.

But he had opened a door and she wanted that door to remain open. She wanted to enter the unexplored room and see what was there…

She stirred on the bed then pushed herself backwards so that she was propped against the pillows, which she arranged under her, her vibrant blonde hair tangled around her flushed face.

Dio was her husband yet she felt as tongue-tied as a teenager on her first date with the cutest boy in class.

'Why are you just standing there?' she challenged, dry mouthed. 'Isn't this what you wanted? To carry me up here so that you could get *what you paid for*?'

Dio flushed darkly and scowled. Was that how he had sounded? Like a thug?

'Nearly a year and a half with no sex, Lucy. Are you

telling me that I got a fair deal when I married you?' His voice was harsher than he had intended and he saw her flinch.

'Maybe neither of us got much of a fair deal.'

Personally, Dio thought the deal she had ended up with had been a hell of a lot better than his.

'You haven't answered my question.'

'You brought me up to your room for sex and here I am. You're getting what you paid for!' Brave words, but the way she cleared her throat alerted Dio to the fact that she might be talking the talk, but that was where it probably ended.

It seemed just one more thing that wasn't fitting into the neat slot he had shoved her into for the past year and a half.

A cold, opportunistic woman would surely not have been able to replicate the nervous wariness he could see beneath the brave statement of intent?

Her fingers wouldn't be digging into her arms to stop them from trembling…

'I find that I'm not as much into self-sacrificing martyrs as I had imagined,' Dio said, pushing himself away from the window ledge against which he had been leaning.

'Even the ones you forked out good money to buy?'

'You were never that cynical, Lucy.' He had a vivid image of her laughing at him with genuine, girlish innocence, the sort of girlish innocence that had made him lose his mind. She might not have been quite as innocent as she had pretended but she certainly hadn't been as sharp-tongued as she was now.

'I grew up,' she said with painful honesty.

'You can run along,' he told her, reaching to the top

button of his shirt. 'I've had a long flight. I'm tired. I'm going to have a shower and hit the sack.'

She didn't want him to.

She could play the passive victim and scuttle off but she wasn't going to do that. She felt as though she had spent the past year or so playing the passive victim—had spent practically *her whole life* playing the passive victim—and now would be her only window in which to take control of a situation.

'What if I decide that I don't want to run along?' she asked with considerable daring.

Dio stilled, hand still poised to remove his shirt. Her chin was mutinously jutting out and he smiled, reluctantly amused by the expression on her face: stubborn, holding her breath, eyes squeezed tightly shut..

'What are you saying?'

'You know what I'm saying.'

'I like things to be spelt out in black and white. No room for error then…'

'I've wondered, okay?'

'Wondered what?' He was standing right by the bed now, looking down at her with a smile of male satisfaction.

'What it would be like…you know…? With you…'

'Even though you've spent many months being an ice-queen?'

'I've been very friendly with all your clients.'

'Maybe I've been longing for a few of those smiles to be directed my way,' Dio murmured. He slowly began unbuttoning his shirt, watching her watching him as his brown chest was exposed inch by inch.

Lucy was riveted. How long had she wanted this? How had this insane desire been so successfully hidden under layers of resentment and simmering anger, with a large dose of self-pity thrown in for good measure?

She watched as he tugged the shirt out from the waistband of his trousers, drew in a deep breath and held it as he shrugged off the shirt altogether, tossing it casually on the ground.

'So, you're curious…' He felt as though he was suddenly walking on clouds. It was an extremely uplifting sensation. In fact, when it came to the feel-good factor, this was as good as it got. Her eyes were huge and, yes, curious. He was bulging in his trousers, thick and hard and desperate for a release, which he was going to take his time getting to.

Drugged by the sensational vision of him half-naked… her bronzed god of a soon-to-be ex-husband… Lucy was deprived of speech. She nodded and didn't even bother trying to tear her eyes away from his glorious body.

'I confess I'm curious too,' Dio admitted, basking in her undiluted fascination with his body. 'So it's time for you to return the favour…'

'Huh?' Lucy blinked.

'One good turn deserves another,' Dio said drily. 'Or, in this case, one semi-striptease deserves another.'

'You want me to…?'

'We're man and wife.' He gestured broadly. 'A little bit of nudity should be as nothing between us.'

'I hate it when you do that,' she complained. He grinned and that grin erased all the forbidding, harsh lines of his beautiful face; made him seem almost boyish.

'Do what?'

'Oh, don't play the innocent with me.' But she smiled shyly and sat up. Her fingers were shaking; her hands were shaking. He had no idea that she had never done anything like this in her life before. Okay, at university there had been some good-natured fumbling with the two boys she had dated for six months and three months respectively. But they'd been boys and he was…

Dio…

Nerves ripped into her with a vengeance, but she had committed to this path, *wanted* this path, and she wasn't going to give in to cold feet now.

But that didn't mean that she wasn't shaking like a leaf as she dragged the tee-shirt over her head and flung it to the ground where it joined his shirt.

He had folded his arms and was staring, just as though she really was performing a proper striptease for his benefit only.

Which, she supposed, she was, in a way.

She closed her eyes, reached behind, unclasped her bra and, still with her eyes shut, flung the bra onto the little growing heap of discarded clothes.

'You can open your eyes,' Dio drawled. He was surprised he could talk at all because the sight of her was enough to take his breath away.

He loved the way she was sprawled there on his bed, her head averted. He could see the tiny pulse beating in her neck and, God, he wanted to fall on her, take her, sate himself with her body.

She was beyond captivating.

Pale, slender, her small breasts pert and pointed, her nipples as pink as he had imagined, but bigger. Perfect, circular discs that sent his blood pressure soaring.

Lucy opened her eyes and slid a hesitating, self-conscious sideways glance at him. She had no idea where she had found the courage to do what she had done, but she had had to do it, and one look at the naked hunger and desire in his eyes was enough to restore every scrap of her wavering self-confidence. She glanced at his trousers, then back to his face, and he laughed.

'So my beautiful ice-maiden thaws…' He slowly unlooped his belt from his trousers and then pulled down his zipper. He was utterly confident when it came to his own nudity and he really liked the way she was still looking at him. He pulled down the trousers and his boxers in one easy movement, and her eyelids fluttered as she took in the impressive girth of his erection.

'Your turn now…and then you can touch…' He loosely held himself and noted her quick, sharp intake of breath. Just one more of those little hot reactions and he knew that he wouldn't be responsible for what happened next.

Their eyes held and she wriggled her jeans down until she was left only in her panties. She couldn't stop looking at his big hand holding himself.

'Let me feel you first,' Dio said raggedly. He reached down and slipped his hand to cup the moist mound between her legs, then he pushed his finger in before sliding it along the slippery slit until he felt the throbbing nub of her clitoris.

Lucy gave a long, low groan and parted her legs.

There was no room in her head to contemplate her absolute lack of experience.

He would find out soon enough…

CHAPTER SIX

DIO STRADDLED HER and for a few seconds he just looked down at her. His fingers were wet from where he had touched her and felt her excited arousal.

She still seemed unable to meet his eyes in the shadowy darkness of the room and he gently tilted her face so that she was forced to look at him. He wanted to take her fast and hard...he was so aroused that he could scarcely breathe...but he could sense her nerves and, with a sigh, he lay down alongside her then hitched himself up on one elbow.

'Tell me you're not in the grip of second-thought syndrome,' he murmured, stalling her attempts to cover herself with his duvet.

Lucy's burst of self-confidence was fading fast. Her husband was the most beautiful man she had ever laid eyes on and, having spent far too long fantasising about him, she was even more bowled over at his beauty in the flesh. No fantasy could do him justice. He was a man in the very peak of his prime. No part of his impressive body was untoned. His stomach was washboard-flat, his shoulders broad and muscled. His sheer perfection not only made her teeth chatter with nerves but also made her very, very much aware of her lack of experience.

He would have slept with countless women. You could tell that just from the way he was so comfortable in his own skin. He was a man who didn't mind women feasting their eyes on him, who probably enjoyed it.

She didn't imagine that *his* teeth were chattering with nerves at the thought of hopping into the sack with her.

She had to fight off the urge to leap off the bed and make a sprint for her clothes on the ground.

'No, of course I'm not,' she said, dry-mouthed. If he'd been short-tempered or impatient at her sudden shyness, she might have found sufficient anger to rally her mental forces and shrug off her attack of nerves. But his voice was low and curiously gentle and it reached something deep inside her that she hadn't revealed in the long months of their marriage.

Something vulnerable and hesitant. Gone was the hard veneer she had manufactured to protect herself.

'Then why the sudden reticence?' He traced the circle of her breast, running his finger in a spiralling motion until he was outlining her luscious pink nipple. He watched it stiffen and lowered his head to flick his tongue over the toughened nub.

Lucy took a dragging breath and stifled a groan.

'I… I just never thought that we would find ourselves in this situation,' she confessed, expecting the barriers that had existed between them to shoot back into place but, when he replied, his voice was pensive.

'Nor did I, not that I didn't want it.'

'I'm afraid,' she laughed nervously. 'The package without clothes might not be exactly what you'd expected.'

'What makes you say that?'

'I'm not the most voluptuous woman on the planet,'

she said lightly. 'Too flat-chested. When I was at school, and all the other girls were developing breasts and hips, I just developed height and everything else stayed the same. I barely need to wear a bra. Men like women with big boobs. I know that.'

'You know that, do you?' He teased her throbbing nipple with his tongue and felt her melt under his touch.

'Yes. I do. Why else do you think those men's mags have always been so popular?'

'I can't say I've ever given it a passing thought. I've never read those things. What's the point of looking at a picture of a woman when you could be lying in bed with one?' Dio told her truthfully. He hadn't actually banked on doing a whole lot of talking in this arrangement. He had wanted the body she had deprived him of. And since when had sex involved long, soul-searching conversations?

Certainly they never had with him.

In fact, before Lucy, women had been pleasant interludes in a hectic, stressful work life. He had never become emotionally attached—had never encouraged any woman to think that he was, had never given any of that a passing thought. Meaningful conversations had been thin on the ground.

Against all odds, considering she should have been the last woman on earth he would want to have any sort of relationship with, Lucy had been the one woman to lodge underneath his skin. He had never delved deep into asking himself why that was. He had assumed that it was because she was also the one woman who hadn't made bedding him a priority.

Which—and why wouldn't this have been a natural conclusion?—was why he wanted her; why he had been unable to treat the marriage as the sham it had turned out to be and carry on playing the field. It had irritated the hell out of him that she had not given a damn one way or another whether he fooled around or not during their marriage and that, in turn, had been a source of slow-burning anger and dissatisfaction.

Now that she was within reach and he could see that burr under his skin finally being dislodged, he thought that conversation was the least he could do.

If she wanted to talk, then why not?

He couldn't, however, understand the self-denigration. Where had *that* come from? She had led a pampered, privileged life, the only child of wealthy parents. True, her father had been no better than a common criminal, but that didn't nullify all the advantages she had had.

She was, literally, the golden girl. Seeing her in action over the past year or more had really shown him just how easy she found those social graces; just how at home she was moving in the circles which he had been denied, thanks to her father.

He couldn't care less because he had made it to the top but he couldn't seriously credit that the self-confidence she had always oozed was anything but bone-deep.

He wondered where she was going with this and reluctantly was curious to find out.

He kissed the corner of her mouth and she squirmed and manoeuvred her body so that they were facing one another.

'Have you any idea how tough this is for me?' Dio asked her roughly and Lucy blushed.

'What?'

'Feeling your sexy little body pressed up against me. No, I take that back. I think you have a very good idea of how tough this is for me because you can feel my desire against your skin. That says it all.'

'You're…you're very big,' Lucy whispered, and Dio grinned.

'I'll take that as a compliment.'

'I mean…have you ever found that a problem?'

Dio frowned. 'What are you talking about? Why would I have found that a problem? A woman's body is engineered to accommodate a man of my size.'

'There's something I feel you ought to know,' she whispered, heart beating fast. 'I'm not as experienced as you probably think I am.'

'I never thought you were the sort of woman to sleep around.'

'I'm not. In fact, actually, I haven't slept around at all,' she admitted awkwardly and Dio edged back from her.

'Are you telling me that you've never made love to a man before?'

'It's not that big a deal,' she returned defiantly.

Dio remained silent for so long that she wondered whether he was trying to concoct an excuse to withdraw from the situation which he had been so keen to engineer.

'How come?'

'I don't feel comfortable having this conversation. I just thought that…that it was something you should know before…well…' She laughed nervously. 'When you're disappointed, then you'll understand why.'

Dio sat up.

His wife was a virgin. Incomprehensible. How had she managed to withstand the advances from men, looking the way that she did? *Why* had she? He raked his fingers through his hair then swung his legs over the side of the bed.

Lucy took advantage of the moment to yank the duvet over her.

This was a nightmare. What on earth had possessed her? Dio was a man of experience, a guy who had married her as something convenient that came as part of the package deal. He wasn't into virgins and he certainly wouldn't be into holding her hand while she lost her virginity.

She must have been mad.

Mortification swept over her in a hot wave.

Typically, he hadn't bothered to get dressed. While she had felt an urgent need to cover herself, he was as comfortable having this hideous conversation in the buff as he would have been in one of his hand-made Italian suits. He had moved to sit in the chair by the mahogany desk by the bay window.

'How come?' he repeated. 'And please don't tell me again that you don't feel comfortable having this conversation.'

'It just never happened for me.' Bright patches of colour delineated her cheekbones.

There was no way she intended pouring her heart out with some little-girl story of how unhappy her childhood had been; how she had witnessed her mother's miserable stoicism in the face of her father's selfishness and philandering. She wasn't going to drone on in a self-pitying manner about her lofty determination only to have sex with the man she truly loved which, frankly, would have been a confession too far—especially considering the man she had thought she loved had turned out to be just the kind of man she should never have got mixed up with in the first place.

'No testosterone-filled boys creeping through the windows of your prim and proper boarding school to have their wicked way with the innocent virgins?'

His lightly teasing tone was so unlike him that she felt herself begin to relax.

'None of that. There was always the house mistress on red-hot alert, waiting with a rolling pin for any daring intruders.'

She lowered her eyes but could still feel him staring thoughtfully at her and she didn't like that. It made her feel exposed.

'And I suppose daddy was just as protective with his little girl?' His voice was hard-edged.

Lucy shrugged. Yes, he'd seen off potential boyfriends all right, not that there had been many of them, but only because he had been such a crashing snob that no one had fitted the bill.

In retrospect, taking into account his dire financial situation, none of them had had the necessary bank balances to provide a rescue package anyway. Dio had certainly fitted the bill and he had not been on her father's ridiculous social-climbing radar.

Watching her, Dio saw a shadow cross her face, gone as quickly as it had come, and he was struck by a sudden intense curiosity to find out what lay behind that shadow.

'I would completely understand if you'd rather call it a day right now.' She laughed a little unsteadily. 'It was a stupid idea, anyway. You can't just *have a honeymoon* and pretend that all the stuff that's happened between us never took place.'

'You'd be surprised,' Dio murmured.

He stood up and strolled over to the bed. She was a virgin. The thought rocked him, brought out a fierce possessiveness which he never knew he had. All those nervous little looks and shy glances now made sense. He'd never have guessed, but then he hadn't been looking, had he? He had accepted the cover version of her, the cool, elegant woman born into wealth and comfortable with it.

He hadn't thought to look any deeper. She had deceived him, as far as he was concerned, that that was the end of the story. He had closed the door and it had been a lot easier to keep it closed.

'I'm surprised,' he murmured, 'to think that you have never made love to a man before...shocked, even...but not turned off. I have no idea where you got that notion from, my dearest wife.'

His voice was low and husky, his grey eyes glittering with intent.

'But can I ask you one thing?' He returned to the bed, depressing the mattress with his weight, and very slowly pulled down the duvet which she had dragged up to her neck in a vain attempt at modesty. 'Why choose the husband you're keen to divorce? Seems an unusual option.'

Lucy felt that if he listened hard enough he would be able to hear the steady, nervous thump of her heart.

Now, wasn't *that* a question?

'I fancy you.'

'And fancying me is enough to paper over the fact that you don't like me?'

Lucy felt that she could say the same about him, but men were different from women, weren't they? Women looked for love and men sought sex. That was why Dio had never been tempted in the past to hitch his wagon to any of the many women he had slept with. There had been no broken engagements or heart-rending tales of thwarted love. When they had been dating, during that brief window when she had actually believed that he was interested in her for herself, he had laughed when she had asked him whether he had ever been in love.

Dio might have used her, and certainly did not feel anything for her, not even affection—but he would still have no problem getting into bed with her because, as far as he was concerned, that was part of the marriage contract which he had been denied and, besides, he didn't think she was half bad-looking.

It was slowly dawning on her that she might hate him for stringing her along—might hate that core of coldness inside him that had allowed him to be the kind of man who could do that—but there was still something deep in the very heart of her that wasn't quite as immune to him as she would have liked to be.

She would rather have chewed her own arm off than ever admit that to him.

'Why not?' she asked.

Dio frowned. Their marriage had been little more than a business transaction and he wasn't sure why he now found her attitude unsettling.

'I was young when I married you, Dio. I'm only twenty-four now. Before you came along, I was totally wrapped up doing my maths degree and it didn't leave a whole lot of time for men.'

'You mean I was the first guy you really ever fancied…'

'You're a good-looking man.'

To his ears, that sounded like agreement, which made him wonder why she had retreated to her ivory tower the second the ring was on her finger.

'Then why wait until now?'

'Because maybe I've discovered that I'm more like you than I wanted to admit, even to myself.' She breathed with the panicked sensation of someone treading on thin ice.

So much safer when she had been able to keep her distance and set aside all the uncomfortable thoughts now besieging her.

'Now that we're going to be getting a divorce—'

'That's a matter that's still up for debate…'

'I know the conditions and I accept them,' Lucy told him bluntly. And then she added for good measure, for just that little bit of protection, 'And you're right—I can't see a way forward if I leave this marriage with nothing. I've never known what it was like to be broke.'

'Because Daddy protected you even when he was going under and all but waving a white flag…'

'Whatever.' She took a deep breath and did her utmost to disconnect from the contempt she felt for a man who had betrayed her mother and herself for pretty much all of his life. 'Now we're going to part company for ever in a couple of weeks' time, why deny the fact that I find you an attractive man? It makes sense to sleep with you, Dio. Like you said to me, it won't be a hardship.'

Pretty much everything she said got on Dio's nerves even though there was not a single thing he didn't agree with, not a single thing that shouldn't have eased his conscience.

'And what if I told you that you could have the money you want without the sex?' he heard himself ask.

Lucy looked at him, surprised.

'You mean that?'

'What if I told you that I did?' For a man who didn't deal in hypotheses, he discovered that he was a dab hand at dishing them out. He had seen nothing wrong with going after what he wanted, *what he was owed*, and likewise he had seen nothing wrong in using whatever tools were at his disposal to get there. After all, he owed nothing to a woman who had been his wife in name only for reasons that had suited her at the time. Why should he care about a woman who had turned out to be no better than a gold-digger?

Annoyingly, it now irked him to think that she was only going to hop into bed with him because he had dangled that money carrot in front of her. So she fancied him. Big deal. From the age of thirteen he had known what it was like to be fancied by the opposite sex. But did she fancy him enough to sleep with him if she didn't think that it made financial sense?

He loathed the direction his thoughts were taking but seemed unable to stop the flow now that it had begun.

'Are you? Because, if you're just speculating, then I don't want to be having this conversation. You're free to walk away cash in hand, Lucy, and you don't have to sleep with me as part of the deal.' He flung himself onto his back and stared up at the ceiling. If this was what it felt like to be the good guy, then he could say in all honesty that he'd felt better.

'Really?'

'Feel free to show your true colours, my beloved wife,' Dio said acidly, still staring up at the ceiling but conscious of her naked, sexy body next to his with every treacherous pore of his being.

'I meant what I said when I told you that I want to sleep with you—money doesn't have anything to do with it.'

Dio inclined his head to look at her. He couldn't credit the soar of triumph that greeted her unsteady admission.

'Is that the sound of you telling me that you're using

me…?' He shifted so that he was lying on his side and lost himself in a shameless observation of her beautiful body, even though it was costing him not to touch that beautiful body. Yet.

'And what would you say if I told you that I was?'

'I'll live with it,' he murmured. 'Now, lie back. I don't think I've ever had so much talk before sex in my life before.'

Lucy's eyelids fluttered and she obeyed, sprawling with feline satisfaction, arching slightly so that her small breasts were pushed up.

With an unsteady groan, Dio planted a trail of kisses along her neck, then lower across her collarbone. He found heaven when he finally took one nipple into his mouth. It was sweet and succulent and he suckled on it, feeling it tighten in his mouth and hearing her moan as he swirled his tongue across the sensitive surface before drawing it long and deep into his mouth once again.

Gently he cupped her other breast, massaging it, and then rolling his fingers over her nipple, a warm-up for his mouth.

It was pure agony taking his time but he refused to let himself forget that she was a virgin. His virgin. His virgin bride. The thought of that fired him up on all fronts and appealed to the very essence of his masculinity.

He took his time as he straddled her, pushing her legs wide open to accommodate him, and gently stilling her instinct to snap them shut.

He was so aroused that he could scarcely breathe. If he began telling her what he wanted to do with her, he knew that he would find it impossible not to come.

This was a first for her and in some ways it was a first for him as well. The slight tremble which he knew she was trying hard to contain gentled his natural raw instincts.

Her other nipple was waiting for him and he took it gently into his mouth and teased and licked and sucked until she was writhing underneath him, arching up, her fingers curled into his hair so that she could push him down against her breast.

Her nipple was taut and glistening as he finally drew away. Hands flat on either side of her, he continued to trace a path along her rib cage, over her stomach, pausing to circle her belly button and then lower still…

Lucy's eyes flew open as his mouth moved to caress her inner thigh.

'Dio…'

He looked up and smiled. 'Dio…what…?'

'I… I…'

'Relax. Trust me. You're going to enjoy me kissing you down there.' The scent of her filled his nostrils. 'And don't close your eyes,' he commanded. 'I want to know that you're watching me when I begin licking you…'

Lucy moaned as her imagination took wonderful flight. She was so wet for him, wanted him so much. She marvelled that she had spent so many months primly keeping her distance, little knowing that he had the power to melt every bone in her body until she was as pliant as a rag doll.

She watched as he settled between her legs, hands against the soft flesh of her inner thigh preventing her from closing her legs, making sure that she was open for him.

Delicately he slid his tongue between the soft folds, finding the throbbing bud of her roused clitoris with ease and tickling it.

The pleasure was exquisite.

She wanted to keep her eyes open so that she could see his dark head moving with purpose between her legs but she couldn't. She tilted her head up and arched her back, an instinctive response to what he was doing.

When he plunged his finger into her, whilst keeping up the insistent pressure of his tongue on her clitoris, Lucy could no longer hold herself back.

The waves of pleasure were too much, far too much. She didn't want this…she wanted him in her… But with a long, shuddering groan she gave in to the ripples that increased into an unstoppable riptide of her orgasm.

She came against his mouth, rising up, crying out, moving wildly as his tongue continued its ruthless plunder.

Her own lack of experience stared her in the face as she gradually came back down to earth.

'I'm sorry.' She turned away as he moved up to tilt her chin gently so that they were looking at one another.

'Only tell me you're sorry if you didn't enjoy it.'

'You know I did,' she whispered. 'But I… I should have been able to hold off. I shouldn't have come…not like that…not when I want you in me…'

'I wanted to bring you to an orgasm, Lucy. This is just the foreplay…'

'It's pretty mind-blowing,' Lucy returned shakily.

'You're so beautiful and wet that I'll be able to slide into you, and I'll be gentle. I don't want to hurt you.'

Lucy found it remarkable that this powerful, ruthless man, accustomed to getting his own way at all costs, could be so tender between the sheets.

Yet, wasn't that the hallmark of the expert lover? That was what she told herself because it was bad enough that he was climbing out of the box into which she had securely placed him. She just didn't need yet another side of him to hit her in the face and overturn yet more preconceptions.

He said that she should trust him and that he didn't want to hurt her but some little voice inside cautioned her that it was within his power to deliver a great deal of hurt.

He already had! Surely the proof of the pudding was in the eating? He had married her so that he could socially elevate himself. Her father had been cruelly clear on that count. He had turned her into the cynical woman she was now! It would be wise to remember those things. She knew that the most important thing in the world was self-preservation.

She wanted a divorce, wanted to rid herself of a marriage that was a joke, and tellingly he hadn't argued against that. He wanted her but, once he got that out of his system, he would be more than ready to ditch her and move on with his life, find himself some woman he actually had feelings for and wanted to settled down and have children with.

That woman would never be her.

But, Lord, it was hard to marshal her thoughts when her whole system was in crazy free fall!

She felt him nudge against her and, just like that, a slow burn began. She wrapped her arms around him, loving the hardness of his body.

'Tell me what to do,' she whispered. Those were words that Dio had never heard from any woman and they were curiously thrilling.

'Do nothing but what feels good for you, and lose yourself, Lucy. It's what making love is all about.'

That sounded like a pretty scary concept to her but

she nodded obediently and then stopped thinking altogether as he began to kiss her, slowly, taking his time.

She could taste herself as their tongues meshed. She reached down to hold him; he was massive, a hard shaft of steel that sent her senses spinning.

But she wasn't scared. She knew that he was going to be gentle.

And she wasn't filled with regret either. So what if this didn't make sense? So what if he had offered her the way out she had asked for without the blackmail? He had told her that she could walk away and that she wouldn't walk away penniless and she believed him.

But walking away would have opened the door to, if not regret, then a life of wondering what this husband of hers would have been like in bed, what it might have been like to have touched him.

No. She was doing the right thing.

He cupped her breast and played with it, idly stroking her roused nipple while he remained kissing her until she felt like she was drowning.

Then slowly, oh, so slowly, his hand smoothed over her stomach to cup the mound between her legs. Only then did he caress her down there, but so lightly that she had all the time in the world for her body to crank back into full gear, until she was throbbing and aching for more.

She wanted to push his hand in deeper, but instead she twisted so that she could taste him.

She'd never done anything like this before. She took him into her mouth and heard his sharp intake of breath as she began to lavish attention on the rigid shaft. She ran her tongue exploratively along it, sucked it, filling her mouth; cupped him between his legs and felt him expand under her attentions.

This time, he was the one spiralling out of control, but he pulled back before she could do what he had done to her and bring him to an orgasm with her mouth only.

Their bodies were slick with perspiration.

'Don't be nervous,' he whispered as he settled between her legs.

'I'm not nervous.' She felt the thickness of his erection and shivered with a mixture of wild excitement and apprehension.

'No?'

Lucy heard the amused disbelief in his voice and some of her apprehension drained away. 'Okay. Maybe a little.' Though he was someone whose very being posed a threat—who could be daunting and intimidating; whose presence she had contrived to avoid as much as possible from the very instant she had overheard that conversation on her wedding night—she trusted him wholly and completely with her body.

'You're so wet,' he murmured unsteadily, barely able to control his shaking hands as he blindly reached for protection in the little drawer by the bed, fumbling like an amateur. He nudged into her, feeling her tightness expand to hold him and fighting against a natural urge to ram himself in her right up to the hilt. 'You're going to enjoy everything I do…'

'I already have,' Lucy confessed honestly. She sensed him taking his time and knew that it must be difficult for him. She didn't think that her husband was at all accustomed to taking his time with anything if he wanted it badly enough. It just wasn't in his nature. But he was taking his time now, gently probing deeper, but making sure to ease out before continuing to penetrate her in little stages.

'I like that.' He whispered things in her ear, sexy things he wanted to do with her, that had her blushing to her hairline. With each nudge, her nerves dissipated until she was desperate to feel all of him in her, desperate for the surge of his formidable strength inside her.

With the intuition of experience, Dio felt the change in her and offered a prayer of thanks because holding back was sheer torture.

He thrust deeper and more firmly inside. Rearing up on both hands, unable to hold back any more as he gazed down at her small, perfectly formed breasts, Dio moved with assurance, building up a rhythm until each thrust took her closer and closer over the edge.

Lucy had never thought that sex could feel so good. He'd been right. He had fitted into her as perfectly as a hand fitted into a glove; had fitted into her as though their bodies had been crafted to slot together. And now...

Her fingers dug into the small of his back as he continued to thrust, deeper and deeper, until she felt as though they were fusing into one. It was indescribable.

She hurtled over the edge in a wave of pure ecstasy. There was no room in her head for thought or analysis. Pure sensation took over. Every part of her body was on fire, soaring high, swooping thrillingly, until at last the crashing waves of pleasure became ripples and finally subsided, leaving her limp and utterly sated.

She clung shamelessly to him as he withdrew. Her mind was still in a whirl. She couldn't think straight; her body was tingling and burning and as weak as a kitten.

'Enjoyed?' Dio didn't immediately feel his usual compulsion to vacate the bed the second love-making had come to an end but, then again, he told himself that it wasn't every day he made love to a virgin who also happened to be his lawfully wedded wife.

'It was lovely.'

'Lovely?' He gave a low growl of laughter and swept her damp hair away from her forehead. 'I prefer sensational…' And she had come to him without any pressure at all. Triumph made him heady with renewed desire.

'So, I guess that now we've…made love…' She shifted to disentangle herself from his embrace and he tightened his grip.

It had been easy not to think when she had been caught up in the wonder of making love but now reality began to drip in.

This was her first time and, yes, sensational was definitely the word to describe the experience. But for him this was all routine stuff. He had already given her a time limit of a fortnight, after which he anticipated getting bored, but perhaps she should establish a bit of cool and restraint herself. She'd acted like a limpet and the last thing she wanted was for him to get the idea that this strange situation was one that was out of her control.

Out of control were her physical responses. But that was where it ended.

She wasn't the foolish romantic she'd once been. She'd toughened up.

'Yes?'

The low timbre of his voice was a drag on her senses. 'Would you say we've put this thing between us to rest?' She chuckled lightly.

'What do *you* think?' Dio murmured. He'd been prepared to do the decent thing and let her escape with the money she wanted but things had changed since that bout of decency. He curved his hand possessively between her thighs and felt the slick moisture between her legs.

'You had your chance to fly away, my dearest wife, and you decided not to. Well, fair's fair, wouldn't you say? Ten days of happily wedded bliss and then we part company. Like I've said to you, Lucy, it won't be a hardship for either of us...'

CHAPTER SEVEN

LUCY GAZED DOWN as the plane dipped below the clouds and a vision of glittering blue water dazzled brightly up at her.

Originally, Dio said, he had thought about taking her on safari but had decided that a week and half making love in the sun was a far better idea.

'Why let some lions and elephants interrupt our journey of discovery?' he had drawled, catching her eye and holding it. 'Activity holidays are all well and fine but the only activity I want to do with you involves a bed and not much else...'

Heady stuff, she had thought with a strange pang.

The journey of discovery had not been the one she had contemplated in those giddy days before they had tied the knot. This journey of discovery would be a physical journey, and the only thing they would be discovering would be each other's bodies, but she had been utterly unable to resist.

After that first session of making love, they had made love again and again. Ingrained habit had propelled her out of his bed in the early hours of the morning but he had pulled her back to him and told her that he wanted to wake up next to her in the morning.

She had stayed and they had made love again in the morning, taking their time.

She found it almost impossible to keep her hands off him but she had uneasily given herself permission.

This was an arrangement of sorts, just as their marriage had been.

He could disconnect and so could she. It might not be in her nature but the option of walking away felt as impossible as climbing Mount Everest barefoot.

So the honeymoon that had never happened was arranged without delay. Given that he would then disappear off to the other side of the world to return to his high-octane life of big deals and even bigger money, time was of the essence for him, she guessed.

He had his catching up to do before she was dispatched without a backward glance.

They would be going to his place in the Caribbean. It was one of the few houses which Lucy had not had to personally see to as it hadn't been used since they had married. It was not on the map when it came to entertaining clients. Townhouses and apartments in city centres always received a lot more use.

'Excited?' Dio snapped shut his computer and devoted his attention to his wife, now that the plane was about to land.

He had worked for the duration of the journey even though he had felt her next to him, her floral scent filling his nostrils and driving him to the insanity of joining the Mile High Club.

The sex was going to be explosive. In fact, he couldn't wait to get her into bed again. If he had his way, they wouldn't make it as far as the private beach that surrounded his villa.

That said, he had no intention of losing perspective on this little episode, and keeping a firm hand on the situation was imperative. Raw physical instincts were all well and good provided they obeyed the order he had always imposed on himself. Work first.

'I've never been to the Caribbean before,' Lucy admitted.

'Never?' Dio was astounded.

'In fact, we didn't do a great deal of travelling at all.' Because, she could have added, that would have been a little too much family time for her father to deal with. For them all to deal with, come to it.

'You surprise me,' Dio murmured. 'I would have thought that you and your family would have been fully signed-up members of the playground of the rich club…'

Lucy shrugged and said lightly. 'Life is full of surprises.'

'As I'm discovering,' Dio breathed.

'So…' She dragged the conversation back to its starting point. 'When you asked me whether I was excited… I am. To see the island and to experience island life.' She had twisted to look at him and as their eyes met she felt a sliver of intense excitement race through her body.

'Is that all that's exciting you?'

Lucy reddened. Her mind shot back to the intimacy of their caresses, the way he had made her body come alive, and she licked her lips nervously. He was probably accustomed to women praising him to the skies but, since she wasn't one of his doting fans, she refused to do that.

'Tell me about your house,' she said a little breathlessly.

'What would you like to know?' Dio drawled, breaking off eye contact. 'It was a celebration purchase when

I made my first million in profit. Since then, I've collected a few more properties along the way, as you know only too well.'

Because I look after them like an employee, Lucy thought. It was a timely reminder of their respective roles and the game they were playing and she was thankful for it.

'And you're right.' She dropped her voice to a husky whisper. 'The island and your house aren't the only things I'm looking forward to…'

Dio laughed appreciatively under his breath. This was more like it. The language of desire was a language he understood.

He was barely aware of disembarking. His head was caught up in all sorts of pleasant images of what he intended doing with her the very second they reached his villa. He had made sure that the place was aired, cleaned and supplied with sufficient food and drink to keep them going for the duration if they decided not to venture out. He had a person out there fully employed, even though their only job was to make sure an empty villa was looked after and unused gardens were kept under restraint.

All in all, he looked forward to smooth sailing and satisfying those physical needs he had foolishly underestimated over the past months.

His remarkably non-existent libido in the company of other women, including women who had done their utmost to distract him, should have sounded a warning bell that he still fancied the hell out of his opportunistic wife.

Life, as she had so succinctly pointed out, was certainly full of surprises—and, though never a man to enjoy the unexpected, he intended to enjoy this particular surprise to the full.

And then…divorce.

It made sense.

He squashed the surge of frustration that greeted that thought. Divorce made sense. He had married her, yes—because he had fancied her; because he had come round to thinking that a wife would be a handy accessory; and, of course, he had taken the company, and to take Robert Bishop's daughter as well had seemed fitting retribution for the wrong that had been done to his father.

But life could hardly be called satisfying for either of them. He had not ended up marrying the woman he wanted to bed. He had ended up marrying a woman who had had her eye to the main chance.

He would be well rid of her.

Once he had cleared her from his system, which was what this little sojourn in the tropics would be about.

The same, he assumed, applied to her.

Having travelled the world, he was blasé about a lot. But now, as they were transported to his villa through small streets lined with the waving fronds of coconut trees, with glimpses of turquoise ocean glittering through the spaces, he had to admit that he had chosen a peach of an island on which to buy his villa.

It was tiny. They could cover it end to end in a handful of hours.

And Lucy…

She was as eye-catching as the scenery, as was her enthusiasm. He had never seen her as excited as this at any of the grand houses which had been at her disposal. She peppered him with questions, face flushed, eyes wide, like a kid in a toy shop.

How the hell had the Caribbean managed to pass her

by? Wasn't that one of the bonuses of leading a pampered life? The long haul, over-the-top holidays?

How had *family holidays* passed her by? Unless Daddy had been too busy drinking and dipping his hands in the coffers to spare the time?

After the gluey, uncomfortable heat of summer in a city, it was balmy here, with a breeze blowing lazily through the swaying fronds of the coconut trees, only just disturbing the exotic colours of the flora.

In the twenty minutes it took for them to reach his villa, they passed three cars and many more people on foot. The economy was exclusively tourism-based, and every so often glimpses of millionaires' holiday mansions flashed past, along with several boutique hotels. They drove through the town centre, which was colourful and without a single department store in sight.

As soon as he had decided where they would be heading, he had got his long-suffering secretary to sort out a wardrobe. It would be waiting for them in the bedroom when they arrived.

New experience, new clothes. Simple as that.

'Wow, Dio. This is...spectacular.' Lucy had never seen anything like it. The villa sprawled in gardens that led down to a private cove. Surrounding the entire house was a broad, wooden-planked verandah with pale, sun-bleached railings and, from the overhanging eaves, baskets of brightly coloured flowers spilled out in a welter of extraordinarily diverse colours. Coconut trees fringed the gardens at the back. She could just about make them out. In front, it was picture-perfect, from the blazing blue of the sky, to the ocean stretching out ahead of them seeming so impossibly close to the lush, tropical gardens leading down to the cove.

She gaped.

'I wish I'd been to this house,' she said a little wistfully. 'It would have made a change from the city apartments and houses.'

'You grew up in London. I took you for an urban girl.'

'My mother's family came from Yorkshire,' Lucy said abruptly. 'She was an only child but she remained close to her cousin after her parents died.'

Standing next to her, staring out at the open ocean, Dio frowned at the sudden edgy tension in her voice.

Was she having second thoughts? he wondered. She had certainly gone back to her formal dress, the suitable attire of a rich man's wife. Slim, silk, loose-fitting trousers, a silk top, discreet items of gold jewellery, make-up.

It irked him.

He didn't want to have a hot ten-day fling with the wife he had known for the past few months. He wanted to spend it with the girl he had confronted in that shabby building in East London.

Was he being greedy?

'So your family holidays were in Yorkshire…'

'Mum and I used to go there often.'

'And stay in the family home?'

'That was no longer available to us. We stayed with Aunt Sarah.'

'I see…' He wondered where her slimy father had been when these trips had been taking place. 'I don't recall you disappearing off to Yorkshire after we married.'

'Well,' Lucy said lightly. 'It's not as though we were around one another twenty-four-seven. A lot of the time you were abroad and, when we *were* sharing the same space, well…'

'Which makes it all the more special that we will be

sharing the same space here…but in quite a different way…'

Lucy didn't imagine that long conversations were going to play much of a part in this 'special way' they would be sharing space. Considering she had always placed such a high value on the quality of the relationship that defined a marriage, considering she had sold herself short and made a horrendous mistake, she still couldn't shake the simmering excitement at what lay ahead for the next ten days.

Since when had she ever been interested in sex for the sake of sex?

It baffled her but she was helpless to do anything about it.

'Shall we go in?' She changed the conversation, wondering whether she should play the sexy kitten he expected. 'I'm dying to see what the villa looks like and I feel rather hot and tired.'

'I'll lead the way.'

Inside was as exquisite as the outside. Wooden floors, soft muslin blowing gently in the breeze through open windows, with pale shutters keeping out the blast of the hot sun, bamboo furniture and a short staircase leading to spacious bedrooms and bathrooms on the landing above the ground floor.

He had had someone come in and make sure the place was ready for immediate occupation, although he had done away with having staff on the grounds while they were here. There was a little Jeep, if they wanted to go into the town or to explore other beaches, and enough food and wine to see them through.

It was paradise for the extremely wealthy and she should have taken it in her stride, for she was well accustomed to the palatial splendour of his other properties, but she was still knocked for six as they did a quick tour of the villa.

There was nothing she didn't adore about it, from the furnishings and the feeling of space and light to the magnificent views and the distant sound of the sea.

They bypassed four huge bedrooms and finally she was standing in the room they would be sharing.

The smiling man who had brought them from the airport had deposited her and Dio's scant luggage on the king-sized four-poster bed and it suddenly hit her…

This was their honeymoon. The honeymoon that had never been. She was with her husband and, even though their union had been a cruel joke, she couldn't stop the piercing thrill that filled her when she turned to look at his darkly sexy face.

The windows in the bedroom were sprawled open and she strolled to stare out, breathing in the wonderful balmy air and enjoying the way the breeze lifted her hair from her face.

'Are you going to survive for ten whole days without staff waiting at your beck and call?' she asked, eyeing him, and then nearly subsiding into a frantic, nervous coughing fit as he began to unbutton his shirt, exposing a sliver of hard, brown chest.

'It's a sacrifice I'm prepared to make because I don't want to have anyone around while we're both here.' He slanted just the sort of wicked smile at her that sent her senses shooting off into la la land. 'Come.'

Lucy walked slowly towards him and fell into his arms. His scent filled her nostrils with the punch of a powerful aphrodisiac. She almost lost it and groaned.

It didn't matter how many times her head was telling

her that this was a pretend honeymoon; right here and right now, it felt *real*.

She wanted this man as though there had been no muddy water under the bridge.

Dio tilted her chin and kissed her, a long, lingering kiss; their tongues meshed and explored each other's mouths.

Lucy clung.

'You must be baking hot in this get-up,' he murmured.

Lucy thought that she was damned hot now and it had nothing to do with the temperature. In fact, the outfit was pretty cool, even though her body was on fire.

'I think we need to bath you…'

'We're going to shower…together?'

Dio laughed with open delight and led her to an amazing wet room in different shades of sand and tan marble. 'Now,' he said briskly. 'Clothes off.'

There was furniture in the bathroom. He proceeded to sit on a clean, lined wicker sofa, legs indolently crossed, half-naked and all rippling muscle and sinew.

This felt very different from the safety of a darkened room.

'I can't.'

'Why not?'

'Stage fright.'

Dio threw his head back and laughed, a full-bodied laugh rich with genuine amusement.

'My virgin bride,' he murmured, his silver-grey eyes roaming appreciatively over her fully clad body. 'How about if I break the ice for you?' In one easy movement, he stood up and undressed, and Lucy watched, fascinated by his utter lack of self-consciousness.

'You make me feel so gauche,' she said nervously as

he walked towards her, all powerful, all aroused and all one hundred percent alpha male.

'Touch me.'

Lucy took his heavy shaft between her slender fingers and a ripple of anticipation almost knocked her sideways. Her breathing quickened and her pupils dilated darkly as she played with him, enjoying the power she felt as he moved in her hand.

He controlled his surging response.

He was realising that he couldn't get within a metre of her without his body going crazy. Maybe it was just the natural after effect of all those months of keeping his distance. He should have handled this situation a hell of a lot sooner, but why go down that road? The fact was that they were here now and he intended to waste no time in exploring every single way he could discover his wife's sexy body.

The fact that she was so innocent was an unbelievable turn on.

'If you're self-conscious about doing a striptease for your husband…' he said unsteadily, holding her hand firm, because any more of what she was doing and he would respond in the only way he knew how '…then allow me to perform the task myself…'

Lucy succumbed. With every touch, she shed a little more of her inhibitions. This was what she had dreamed of when she had enthusiastically accepted his marriage proposal. Nothing had turned out quite the way she had expected, but she was determined to enjoy the physical pleasure he was offering her. Neither of them was looking for more than what was on the table.

They showered under jets of water that felt like warm rainfall. Halfway through, he switched off the jets and explored every inch of her with his hand and his mouth while she stood with the water drying on her, back pressed against the cool tiles, eyes closed, savouring every sweet lick. When he brought his mouth against the damp mound of her femininity, she parted her legs and let his tongue drive her to such dizzy heights that she could no longer contain the scorching orgasm that just seemed to go on and on and on as he kept his mouth firmly pressed against her, tasting her as she came.

The promised wardrobe was waiting for her when they finally made it out of the bathroom. Her body was singing.

'So, I had some clothes brought here for you.' Dio threw open the wardrobe doors and Lucy tentatively peered inside.

One by one she went through the things before turning to him where he lay sprawled on the bed in nothing more than a pair of unbuttoned jeans. His hair was still damp from the shower.

'But these aren't what I'm normally accustomed to wearing.'

Dio raised his eyebrows at her confused expression. 'I didn't think designer labels would be appropriate.'

Lucy tentatively stuck on a pair of small, faded denim shorts and the cropped top which could have come straight out of a department store.

These were the clothes she felt comfortable wearing and always had done. Even when she had been surrounded by money, growing up, designer labels had always made her feel like someone who had to be on show, the perfect doll which her father could parade in front of his chums to give an impression of the perfect family that had been far from the truth.

On the many trips she had made back with her mother to Yorkshire, she had ditched the silk and cashmere and enjoyed the freedom of wearing what she wanted. She had escaped the cloying confines of a life she didn't like and this was what it felt like now. A brief escape before she embarked on a whole different life. She was his wife and yet this felt like stolen time.

She told herself that her husband was a guy who knew what he wanted just as he knew what made women tick.

He wanted her and he was shrewd enough to work out that, yes, sophisticated London glamour would not set the scene for the sort of rapid-fire seduction he had in mind.

But there was still a treacherous part of her that was willing to overlook the cynicism behind his choices.

Not that he would have scoured department stores for the clothes himself. He would have told one of his minions what he wanted and that would have been the sum total of his contribution.

It was good that her head was still working, she thought.

'Nice,' he commented approvingly. 'I liked what I saw when I surprised you at that little club of yours and I like what I'm seeing now.'

'I'm not a puppet and you're not my puppet master.' And wasn't this just another form of him dressing her up for his own purposes?

'Is that what you've thought of me during our marriage? That I've tried to control you?' Dio's pale eyes flicked over her flushed face.

'Haven't you?'

'Most women would slice off their own right arm to be controlled by a man who gives them limitless spending money.'

'Dio, I don't want to argue with you about this. We're not here to…to argue…' They had never spoken as much during their marriage as they had done over the past couple of days and there had been times when Lucy had almost felt…*seduced* into telling him why she had pulled back from him the second the final guest had left on their wedding night. Whatever he thought of her and her father, she had wanted him to see her side of the story. She had had to remind herself that he had used her and that was the bottom line.

He had wanted her father's company, had been in a position to grab it for a knockdown price, and, even though he had certainly put right the wrongs her father had done financially, he had got *her* in exchange—the perfect hostess who could move seamlessly amongst his important clients, who actually *knew* some of them from times past.

She suspected that, had they consummated their marriage, he would have tired of her sexually within weeks and would have set his sights on other women.

Once, just once, she had done an Internet search on him to find out about the women in his past. There had been nothing aside from one photo taken from years and years ago of a curvy brunette clinging and laughing up at him as they emerged from a limo somewhere in New York. He had just signed a record-breaking deal.

That single photo had been enough to tell her the sort of women he was drawn to. It gave credence to her father's malicious taunt that Dio was little more than a jumped-up barrow boy who had made a few bucks and needed a suitable little woman to show off to the world that he'd come good.

She had overheard enough on her wedding night to know, for herself, that he was no saint when it came to manipulating an advantage. She had heard the low, cold intent in his voice when he had told her father that he had his company, and he could personally ruin him, but instead he would have his daughter, so he could count his blessings…

She hadn't needed to hear any more.

'No, we're not,' he told her softly. 'So why don't you come and sit here by me and show me why we're here…?'

'Do you ever think of anything but sex?' But she relaxed a little, pleased to close the door on that uneasy conversation between them.

'I'm finding it hard to in this particular situation,' Dio drawled, watching with satisfaction as she strolled towards the bed, looked for a moment as though she intended to take a flying leap on to the mattress but then gracefully settled next to him, though sitting up with her legs crossed.

'And, by the way, I don't like you referring to my project in East London as some *little club* of mine…' Lucy wondered where that had come from, considering she didn't want contentious subjects to get in the way of this arrangement of theirs.

'Following on from that, I've set things in motion to take care of all the finances there.'

'I know and I should have thanked you.' *But she'd had too much on her mind: him.* It made her cringe. 'Mark phoned just before we left and told me. He was very excited and he's waiting until I return so that we can break the news to the community together.'

'Cosy.' Dio frowned. Did she have a crush on the man, whatever she chose to tell him? 'You didn't mention that he called you.'

'I forgot,' Lucy told him honestly. 'Besides…' She lay

down at a distance next to him until he pulled her against him and curved her so that they were facing one another, bodies pressed together.

'Besides what…?'

'Besides, there's no law to prevent me from talking to Mark, especially as we work together.'

'You can have however many cosy chats you want to have with him, and with anyone else for that matter, once you're no longer my wife.' Dio knew that he was overreacting. The man was a limp-wristed tree-hugger.

Except that was probably just the sort of guy Lucy would be attracted to. In an ideal world.

The thought got on his nerves and he found that he couldn't let it go.

'Who else comprises this little community of do-gooders?' he asked and Lucy tugged herself free of him and lay back to stare at the ceiling.

'Why do you have to be so condescending?'

'I'm not being condescending. I'm expressing curiosity.'

'I would have thought that you, of all people, would have sympathised with *do-gooders* who actually want to do something to help those who aren't so lucky in life.'

'Let's not get into my background, Lucy.'

'Why not?' She looked at him, glaring. 'You always feel free to get into mine.' Not that he knew the first thing about what her background had really been about!

'You're avoiding my question. Who else works with you? How long have you known them? Did you approach these people or did they approach you, via some kind of mutual acquaintance?' Dio heard the rampant possessiveness in his voice with distaste.

Lucy was bewildered at the harshness of his voice. What, really and truly, did he care one way or another?

'I approached them,' she admitted. 'I wanted to do more with my life than just be a hostess looking after your properties and mixing with other women who were married to similarly wealthy men. I wanted to use my brain and I saw an ad online so I applied. And there are a few of us who volunteer on a part-time basis. Mark is the key guy but there are… Well, do you want me to name them all?'

'Like I said, I'm curious. Humour me.'

With a sigh—because she couldn't recall him ever being that curious about what she got up to when he wasn't around and she saw his sudden burst of curiosity as just another controlling aspect of his personality—she listed the five other members of their team: three women, all much older than her, and two guys.

'And, when the cat's away, you socialise with these people?'

'Off and on.'

'Whilst concealing who you really are: no wedding ring in sight…'

'I wanted to be taken seriously, Dio. If they knew… Well, if they knew that I was married to you, that I lived in the house I live in, chances are they would just write me off as some rich young girl playing at helping out. Why are we having this conversation?'

Dio wasn't entirely sure himself. He just knew that nothing she said was filling him with satisfaction. 'So none of those guys know that you're married.'

'Not unless they're physic.'

'And what are they like?' he asked with studied casualness.

Lucy thought about Simon and Terence. 'Really, really nice,' she admitted. 'They're both full-time teachers and yet they still manage to find the time to come in whenever they can. They do at least three after-school classes a week. Simon teaches maths alongside me. Terry covers English and history. I can't wait to break the news about what...what you're going to do about injecting some cash into the organisation. They'll be over the moon.'

'Indeed...' Dio ran his hand along her smooth thigh and felt her quiver in immediate response. 'And, when the delighted celebrations kick off, I think it's only fitting that I attend as the wealthy benefactor...wouldn't you agree?'

Lucy shrugged and tried to imagine her husband mixing with the teachers and parents. She had a mental image of a lion being dumped into a litter of kittens.

But of course he would want to see where his money was going. He wasn't a complete idiot. He might have used that as a way of getting her where he wanted her, but he was shrewd enough not to write off the cash as money that could be blown.

And yet, did she want him invading this very private part of her life? The part of her life that she had mentally linked to her bid for freedom?

A sudden thought occurred to her and it was unsettling. Would he actually want to do much more than just throw money at the project? Would he want to oversee things? Would he still be a presence in her life, a dark, powerful, disturbing presence, even after they were divorced?

'I don't think we should talk about this,' she murmured, reaching down to hold him, feeling a surge of power at being able to distract him simply by touching him. 'I think there are far better things to do than talk right now…'

Dio swept aside the uneasy feeling that, for once, he wasn't entirely sure that he could agree…

CHAPTER EIGHT

OVER THE NEXT few days Lucy successfully managed to suppress those niggling, uncomfortable thoughts that occasionally bobbed to the surface.

What was going to happen once they left this paradise bubble they were in? Would he expect her to leave the house by the time he returned to London after his Hong Kong trip? Would he choose to keep working abroad until the coast was clear? Naturally, they would have to talk about the nitty-gritty business of the divorce. It wasn't something that would happen at the click of his imperious fingers but she had no intention of contesting whatever financial settlement he agreed to give her.

Strangely, the seductive lure of gaining her freedom no longer shone like a beacon at the end of a dark tunnel.

She assumed that that was because she was having the time of her life.

It amazed her, this ability to divorce her emotions from a physical side of her she'd never known she possessed.

It was as though something so powerful had awakened in her that it overrode all her common sense.

Sex. Everywhere and anywhere.

At night, they shared the same bed and, far from that feeling weird and abnormal, it felt absolutely brilliant.

She enjoyed that period of being half-awake, half-asleep, curling into the warmth of his naked body and feeling it stir into instant response.

Everything else took a back seat. Misgivings. Unanswered questions. Simmering resentments. None of it mattered when they were making love. He'd been right. This so-called honeymoon, a time when they could both exorcise whatever it was they had to exorcise, was no hardship at all.

Today, a boat trip had been planned. Lucy looked up at the ceiling, missing the presence of Dio's body next to her because he had awakened at the crack of dawn and was in some other part of the villa working.

A little smile curved her mouth. Before he had left the bed, he had touched her, slipped his finger into her half-slumbering body and brought her to a climax while she had been in a glorious state of semi-sleep. It had been exquisite.

In a second, she would get up, have a shower, change into her bikini, with a wrap over her, and the flip flops which he had also managed to think about including in the wardrobe he had had imported from who knew where.

Right now, though, a nagging headache was sapping her of her energy and she remained in the bed with the overhead fan whirring efficiently over her and an early morning breeze wafting through the open windows.

Under the light sheet and blanket, her body felt hot and achy and she stirred, trying to find a more restful position.

She had no idea that she had fallen asleep until she heard his voice reaching her from a great height. At least, it felt like a great height, booming down into the room, making her feel a little faint.

'You're shouting,' she muttered, not opening her eyes and turning onto her side.

'I couldn't talk any lower if I tried.' Time had run away and it was after nine. Irritated by a pressing physical urge to take the steps two at a time, back up to the bedroom so that they could make love before setting off, Dio had controlled the impulse but now…

He frowned, standing at the side of the bed.

'It's nearly nine-thirty, Lucy…'

'Oh, no.' With a cry of dismay, she sat up and instantly fell back onto the pillow.

'What's wrong?'

'I…nothing; nothing's wrong. Just give me a couple of minutes. I'll get dressed and be down in, er, a little while.'

Everything was wrong, she thought faintly. Just three more days to go of living like this, far away from reality, and what did her body have to go and do? Fall ill!

She was in the grip of an oncoming cold at the very least. At worst, she was going to get the flu with all its nasty, debilitating side effects.

Right now, her head was banging, her limbs felt like lead, her mouth was dry and she knew that she was running a fever. She could feel it in the aching of her joints.

Disappointment speared her.

And if she was disappointed then she shuddered to think how furious Dio was going to be.

This was the honeymoon he had demanded and he had ended up with half of it and—worse—a wife who wasn't well. When she half-opened her eyes it was to find that he was still standing by the bed with a frown.

He reached down and pressed the back of his hand against her forehead.

'Nothing wrong? You're running a fever, Lucy!'

'I'm sorry.' Her reply was half-audible and addressed to his departing back.

She didn't blame him. He was so pissed off about the situation that he had headed back down to do something useful with himself. Like carry on working. Having had to cancel the boat and unravel the picnic hamper which had been delivered especially to the house the evening before.

Misery overwhelmed her. When she thought about leaving the island without having the opportunity to touch him again, she felt sick.

She didn't hear him re-enter the room until she felt his arm under her, propping her up into a sitting position.

He had a thermometer in one hand and a glass of water in the other.

'Why didn't you tell me that you weren't feeling well?'

'Because I was fine last night. I just...woke up this morning with a bit of a headache. I thought it would go away but I fell back asleep and... I'm sorry, Dio.'

Dio impatiently clicked his tongue and sat down on the bed next to her.

Sorry? Did she perceive him as that much of a monster that she would feel the need to apologise for not being well? He considered the way he had held the sword over her head, using the threat of sending her packing penniless as a means to an end. An end which he told himself he more than richly deserved.

He thought of the way he had announced, for all to hear, that renovation of the building that meant so much to them rested on her shoulders, doubly strengthening the case for her to get into bed with him.

He had seen taking her as a right which he had been denied. He had justified everything because she fancied him as much as he fancied her. Two consenting adults, all said and told, so what was the problem with that?

For him, he had had unfinished business and, typically, he had got exactly what he had wanted by using all the tools at his disposal—and gentle persuasion had not been one of them.

He was assailed by a rare attack of guilt and he flushed darkly as he stared down at her.

'I've phoned the island doctor.'

'Why?'

'Let me take your temperature.'

'There's no need! I have a cold, Dio. There's nothing anyone can do about that.'

'Open your mouth. Once I've taken your temperature, I've brought you some tablets.'

'What about the boat trip?' Lucy all but wailed. *What about the rest of our stolen honeymoon?* She was ashamed to find herself thinking about whether she could have some kind of IOU note, promising her three more days of snatched love-making once she was better. She found herself wishing his Hong Kong deal might not require his presence after all.

She found herself being *clingy...*

Appalled, she tried to recapture some of the hard-headed common sense that had been her constant companion for all the long months she had been married to him.

How had she suddenly become *clingy*? Was it because she was ill and far removed from her comfort zone? That line of reasoning at least made her feel a little less panicky.

'The boat trip is the least of your worries right now,' Dio told her drily. 'Now shut up and let me take your temperature.'

He did and then frowned. 'Okay, drink as much water as you can and take these tablets. You're running a high fever, Lucy. It's a bloody good job I called a doctor. He should be here any minute.'

'I told you, it's just a cold…'

'Mosquitoes can carry diseases in the tropics,' Dio said patiently. 'Not malaria, fortunately, but other diseases that can be almost as severe. Now, water—drink.'

Lucy did as she was told then she lay back, perspiring, eyes closed.

'You don't have to stay here, Dio. I know you probably have better things to do than tend to a sick wife.' She smiled but kept her eyes closed. Her words were composed and controlled but her thoughts were all over the place and she still couldn't seem to harness them. As fast as she got one under control, a swarm of others broke their leash.

'Name a few.'

'Work. It's the great love of your life.' She yawned and adjusted her position on the bed.

'It's had to be,' Dio murmured absently. 'When you have to drag yourself up by the boot straps, getting out of the quicksand becomes a full-time occupation.'

'And it's hard to let go,' Lucy said drowsily.

'And it's hard to let go,' Dio echoed, surprising himself by that sliver of confidential information he had passed on to her. 'Right. Don't move. The doctor's here.'

'Move? Where am I going to go? My legs feel like jelly.'

Dio grinned. His wife might have played the part she had been briefed to play perfectly over the past year or more, might have shown up at important events always wearing the right thing and always saying the right things and making the right noises. But he had learned what he had maybe suspected all along—that there was a feisty, stubborn streak to her lurking just below the surface, the same streak that had prompted her to break out of the box into which she had been sealed and look elsewhere for fulfilment.

He couldn't stand the thought of her having to look anywhere else beyond him, yet not only could he understand the urge that had prompted her but he reluctantly admired it.

Most women would never have thought to do anything but enjoy a life of stupendous luxury.

Most women would have slept with him.

He was finding it difficult not to think that there was far more to her than the opportunist working in cahoots with her father.

The doctor was a small, brisk man who bustled up to the bedroom, throwing little facts over his shoulder about germs, bugs and the innumerable things that could happen even on an island as small as theirs.

No snakes, he informed Dio crisply, shaking his head, but who said that mosquitoes couldn't wreak similar havoc?

There was a certain little mosquito…

Dio found himself bombarded with a litany of Latin names as he pushed open the bedroom door and followed the doctor into the room where Lucy was tossing restlessly on the bed, her cheeks bright red, her eyes glazed.

The doctor barely needed to examine her, although he was meticulous, taking his time and shaking his head before pronouncing his diagnosis.

Yet another long Latin term and Dio impatiently asked for clarification.

'Something similar to Dengue fever,' he pronounced, standing up and collecting his bag from the floor. 'Not as serious but nasty enough to wipe your wife out for as long as a week. No antibiotics needed. Just a lot of fluid and a lot of rest. The usual painkillers will do their best to fight the fever and the aching joints but, on the bright side, once it clears her system she'll be immune to catching this particular bug again.'

Lucy was appalled at the diagnosis. Drifting in and out of sleep, she woke as night was drawing in to find that Dio had brought his computer up to the bedroom and was working, keeping an eye on her. He hadn't signed up to any of this. She looked at him miserably. Even furious with her, which he would be, he still managed to draw her eye and hold it and, to his immense credit, he didn't show the annoyance on his face when he caught her staring at him.

'You're about to apologise again,' he drawled. 'Save it. You've caught something unpleasant from a mosquito bite and apologising isn't to make it go away. How are you feeling? You need to drink some more water and have something to eat.'

He stood up, stretched and strolled over to sit on the bed next to her. 'At least you're not so hot that I could cook a meal on you.'

'You're being very nice about this.'

'What would you have me do?'

'You don't have to be, you know. Nice. You don't have to be nice.'

'Are you giving me permission to be the sort of person you expect me to be?' There was an edge to his voice, although his expression was mild.

'This is supposed to be our overdue honeymoon.' Bitterness crept into her voice. 'A honeymoon is no place for getting sick.'

'And, on that note, I shall go and get you something to eat. My instructions are to keep you rested, fed and watered.'

He headed out to the kitchen where he banged his fist on the granite worktop.

How low was her opinion of him? Could it get any lower? This was supposed to have been an uncomplicated few days for him, during which he would get her out of his system the only way he knew how. And yet here he was now, frustrated by her unspoken insinuation that she might find him sexy, but that was as far as the complimentary thoughts went. On every other front, he was the sort of person she would have avoided at all costs.

She had apologised for being ill; had told him that getting ill had not been part of the honeymoon deal.

Was she afraid, deep down, that he would still see it as his right to have sex with her because he had effectively *paid* for it? He was repulsed by the idea.

Fifteen minutes later, he was on his way back up to the bedroom with a tray of food and her eyes opened wide when she took in the plate of bread and eggs and the long glass of fruit juice.

'You cooked this *yourself*?'

'You sound a lot better,' he drawled, setting the tray down on the bed next to her and dragging the chair closer to the bed. 'That sharp tongue of yours was missing in action while you were tossing and turning with a high fever. Headache gone? And yes, in answer to your question, I cooked it myself. I'd give myself a pat on the back if the meal was more complicated than bread and two scrambled eggs. Are you going to thank me profusely and tell me that producing some bread and eggs for you was not part of the honeymoon deal?'

Funnily enough, that had been on her mind, and she blushed and tucked into the food, losing her appetite after a couple of mouthfuls.

She had taken painkillers a couple of hours previously and she could feel all the aches and pains and soaring fever waiting to stage a comeback.

In the meantime…

'Maybe…maybe we should talk about the divorce,' she ventured hesitantly.

When he was touching her, she lost all power to reason or even to string a sentence together coherently. But he wasn't touching her now, *couldn't* touch her now, and she thought that it might be better to talk about the awkward elephant in the room rather than wait until they were back in London, when the barriers would be up again. Strangely, she didn't want to remember her final time with him as a cold war during which their communication was translated via lawyers and would revolve around money. At least if they sorted things out between themselves here in this setting, far removed from reality, they would part company with less bitterness between them.

Dio stiffened. He wondered whether she was making sure to pin him down to the details before the sex was over. Did she imagine that he would walk off into the sunset, having got what he wanted, without completing his half of the bargain? Maybe she thought that being ill had left her vulnerable to him having a rethink about the terms and conditions of their brief affair.

Despite the doubts he was beginning to have about all the assumptions he had made about her, Dio lost no time in allowing his imagination to jump to all the worst possible conclusions.

It was safe territory.

'Feel up to that, do you?'

'I'm not as groggy as I was earlier. I've got an hour or so before the painkillers really begin to wear off.'

'And why not use the time constructively?' He removed the plate of half-finished food, dumped it on the dressing table, returned to his chair by the bed and folded his arms. 'I get where you're coming from.'

Lucy breathed a sigh of relief. Should she try and explain that it would be better to get this awkward situation dealt with and put it behind them, like a boil that had to be lanced so that they could enjoy whatever brief time remained to them?

Or would that confession make her seem foolish? A bit of a loser? Over-sentimental?

And why should she feel sentimental anyway? Was it some lingering after effect of having grown up to be the sort of girl who had believed in the sanctity of marriage? Had there been some part of her that still viewed divorce, whatever the circumstances, as a personal failure?

Even though this particular divorce couldn't happen fast enough…

It just showed how easily led the body was. It could veer off in a wildly different direction from the one the mind was telling it to stick to.

She wondered whether she could get over this stupid bug in double-quick time if she just stayed in bed for the next twenty-four hours. Then they could at least have the last bit of their stay here together…

It would be self-indulgent and probably a very bad idea but why not? And at least if they sorted the whole divorce thing out they wouldn't have that hanging over their heads like the Sword of Damocles...

She could pretend that it didn't exist, just like she had been pretending that this honeymoon wasn't what it really was.

'If you like, I can bring some paper and a pen and put my signature somewhere so that you don't think that I'm going to renege on the deal...'

'I... I just want to know when you'd want me out of the house.'

'This conversation is sordid.'

'Why?'

'You're sick and, even if you weren't, we haven't come here to talk about the details of our divorce. Call me mad but I've always thought that there's nothing more guaranteed to ruin a honeymoon atmosphere than talking about divorce.'

'I just thought...'

'The fact that you've been bitten by a mosquito and ended up in bed ill won't affect your financial package.' Dio knew that that was a brutal way of saying what he wanted to say but he didn't take it back.

Nothing about what they were doing was real but, hell, he was still enjoying it and the last thing he needed was a reminder of just what had propelled her into his bed in the first place.

'I wasn't thinking about the money side of things,' Lucy said faintly.

Dio looked away, mouth drawn into a thin line. 'If there's one thing life taught me,' he said with lazy coolness, 'it's that when someone tells you that the last thing on their mind is money it's invariably the one thing they're thinking about.'

'If you don't want to discuss this then forget it. I just thought that while we're both here it might be better to talk face to face than for us to return to London and have lawyers do it on our behalf. I mean, divorce is a really personal thing.'

'And most divorces usually go down a slightly different route.' He raked his hands through is hair, outraged that she would stubbornly persist with this even though it must be obvious to her that it was an inappropriate topic of conversation. More to the point, it was a conversation he didn't want to be having.

'Most people usually end up facing one another across a desk with lawyers at their sides after they've spent years rowing and arguing. By the time most people hit the divorce courts, they'd tired and fed up of the arguments and they're ready to bow down to the inevitable. That's a personal divorce, one where emotions have been exhausted. This isn't one of those instances.'

'It doesn't make it any less personal.' She thought of her parents and their lousy marriage. There hadn't been years of shouting and arguing, just a quiet destructive undercurrent with insults and criticism delivered in a moderate tone of voice. Unless, of course, her father had been rolling drunk but even then he had never been a crashing around the house kind of drunk. Theirs had been a silent, failing marriage and was nothing like what she and Dio had.

'You're right. It's not.' She stared off into the distance quietly. 'But not all marriages that break down end up that way, after years of shouting and throwing plates. Some marriages just end up broken and useless with no shouting at all. In fact, shouting can be a good thing in a marriage. Anyway, I don't know why we're talking about this…' She shook her head and looked at him, resting back against the pillows. 'I shouldn't have brought this up in the first place.'

She did that.

Opened a conversation in which he had no desire to participate and then got him to a point where his curiosity had been stirred, only to back away, leaving him with a bit between his teeth.

Did she do that on purpose or was it just some fantastic ingrained talent she had managed to hone over the years?

He just knew that he now wanted to find out what she was thinking, why her expression had suddenly become so pensive. He wanted to know what the heck was going through her head.

'What are you going on about?' He placed one finger under her chin and directed her head so that she had no choice but to look at him. 'One minute you're telling me that you want to discuss our divorce so that you can make sure you get your financial settlement—'

'That's not what I said!'

'And the next minute you're generalising about broken marriages where there's no arguing. Are you talking about any marriage in particular?' It was a stab in the dark and he could see, immediately, that he had hit the jackpot. Her eyelids flickered and her mouth parted on some unspoken denial, her fingers compulsively twisting the thin sheet covering her.

'Some friend of yours, Lucy? Aunt? Cousin?' She didn't reply. 'Your parents?' he asked softly, for want of any other name to pull out of the hat, and she gave a terse nod.

Dio was astounded. He drew in a sharp breath and

looked at her narrowly to see whether she was having him on but her eyes were wide and unblinking.

'I've never told anyone before.' Her head was beginning to throb. She closed her eyes, part of her knowing that she should just shut up because the fever and the aching limbs were a potent mix, making her want to say things she knew she shouldn't.

'And there's no need to now,' he murmured, instinctively knowing that once certain doors were opened they could never again be closed, and suspecting that this might just be one of those doors.

Did he want his assumptions overthrown?

Did he want to hear about her parents and their occasional well-bred tiffs? Frankly, when you thought about it, any wife in her right mind wouldn't have been able to stand Robert Bishop for longer than five minutes, because the man was a disaster area.

But the picture he had always had of the Bishop family had been one of the perfect nuclear unit blessed with beauty and wealth all round…

'You probably think that I had a great childhood,' she murmured drowsily. 'Actually, lots of people think that. Well, except for very close family friends and some relatives. Not many.' She slid her eyes over at him and smiled. 'In our circles,' she said with a trace of irony in her voice, 'it doesn't do to wash your dirty linen in public.'

'You should get some sleep, Lucy.'

'Maybe you're right. I guess I should.' She sighed and Dio grudgingly pinned his silver grey eyes to her flushed, rosy face.

'Tell me,' he commanded gruffly.

'Nothing much to tell,' she yawned. 'It's just that… we're going to be getting a divorce and I don't want you to go away thinking that I'm a prim and proper, pampered little princess who was born with a silver spoon in her mouth.'

'Which bit of that statement is not true?'

'You've always thought the worst of me, Dio.'

'God, Lucy. I didn't come over here so that we could end up having long, meaningful conversations about where we went wrong.'

'Because we should just have been out here pretending that we could spend time in one another's company and get through it with sex alone.'

'I thought we were managing just fine on that front.'

With every bone aching, Lucy still felt a crazy quiver at the wolfishness of his smile and the sudden flare of heat in his lean, handsome face.

A mosquito-borne virus made her feel less wobbly than his lazy, brooding eyes.

'I tried hard to forget that you only married me because you figured I would make a suitable wife.'

About to remove the tray of half eaten food on the bed, Dio paused and looked at her narrowly.

Fever made a person semi-delirious and he could tell that her fever was back. However, she sounded calm and controlled, even though her eyes were over-bright and there was a sheen on her face.

'A suitable wife…'

'Right background. You know.'

'Do I?' He sat back down. 'I'm not so sure that I do. Enlighten me.'

Lucy twisted the sheet between her fingers. 'On our wedding night,' she said so quietly that he had to lean forward to catch what she was saying, 'I overheard you talking to my father. Well, more of a heated conversation, to be honest. I heard you telling him that he had got what he deserved and that you were going to make sure that you took what was owed to you. The company…and everything that went with it…'

Dio cursed fluently under his breath as pieces of a jigsaw puzzle slotted into shape. She had heard snatches of conversation; she might have cast her own interpretation on what she had heard, but…

Was he going to provide a fuller explanation? No. He'd wanted revenge. It was something that had eaten away at him since he had been a young adult. He'd got it. But now he felt strangely disconcerted as he questioned that driving passion that had propelled him forward for years.

Stupid.

The man had deserved everything he had got, and not only because of what he had done to his father, but for what he had done to the people who had held shares in the company, the people he had been happy to throw to the wolves by embezzling their money.

So he'd been diverted by Lucy, had married her for not entirely honourable reasons, but her life had been pretty damn good.

Except…

'He told me that you married me because I was the sort of person who could give you social credence, you know. He said that…'

'That *what*…?'

'That you came from a deprived background and what you wanted was someone who could promote your chances to go through doors you wouldn't normally be allowed to go through. That you might have made a lot of money but…but you didn't have…have…what it took to gain entry into certain circles.'

For a few seconds, Dio actually thought that he had misheard her, but as the meaning of her words sank in rage engulfed him.

If Robert Bishop hadn't been safely six foot under, he might have been tempted to send him there.

'And you believed him?'

'Why wouldn't I?' Lucy asked, confused. The dark anger on his face, which he was struggling to control, made her wish that she'd never broached the topic. 'Anyway, I'm beginning to feel really tired. Plus my headache's coming back and the fever...'

Fetching painkillers gave Dio a few minutes during which he suppressed a violent urge to punch something very hard.

Then, just like that, his thoughts veered off in a different direction and he was moderately calmer when he sat back down and watched her swallow the tablets and then lie back with her eyes closed.

'You're not going to fall asleep on me now, are you, Luce?'

Lucy didn't say anything. He hadn't called her that for a very long time, not since they had first started going out; not since they had been on one of those few early dates...

She was aching all over but still alert, fired up by the fact that she had confided in her husband for the first time in many long months. It felt liberating because what did she have to lose?

'When you said that your childhood wasn't what everyone assumed,' Dio said thoughtfully, 'what you really meant was that your father wasn't the man the world thought him to be.'

Her eyelids flickered and she sneaked a glance at him

to see if she could figure out what was going through his head but Dio only ever revealed what he wanted other people to see. She knew that and right now he wasn't revealing anything at all about what he was thinking.

'Was his abuse...physical?' Just voicing those thoughts out loud was sickening but he had to know and he felt a wave of relief when she shook her head in denial.

'He was brutal to me and Mum but it was only ever verbal. My mother was such a gentle creature...'

'So you overheard our conversation and your father convinced you that the only reason I married you was because I wanted to use you to gain social entry to... God only knows where. It never occurred to you that I couldn't give a damn about gaining social entry to anywhere? No...' He pensively provided his own answer to that question before she could confirm his suspicions. 'It wouldn't because he appealed to all your insecurities...' And yet a lifetime of good schools where an ability to mask emotion and project the right image had stood her in good stead when it came to maintaining an air of cool.

'You mean you didn't...use me?'

'I mean...' Guilt seared through him as he trod carefully around his words. 'If you think I married you because you had the right background, or because I thought you could open doors for me, then you're very mistaken.' He stood up, unwilling to go down any further roads, because those roads were riddled with landmines. 'And now, get some sleep, Lucy. Doctor's orders...'

CHAPTER NINE

LUCY WAS VAGUELY aware of time passing by over the next couple of days. The fever came and went in phases, as did the pain in her joints, making her feel as weak as a kitten.

However, when she did surface from the virus, her recovery was swift. She awoke to a room awash with pale light sifting through the closed shutters and the muslin drapes and the soft, overhead whirring of the fan.

A quick glance at the clock by the bed told her that it was a little after eight in the morning. Dio wasn't in the room.

She took time out to mull over certain flashbacks that floated to the surface.

He'd been around all the time. She could remember waking to find him sitting in the room with his laptop at a little table he had brought from some other part of the house. She could remember him bringing her food, which had been largely left uneaten, and making her drink lots of fluids. He had bathed her and helped her with whatever she had needed.

He hadn't signed up to look after her. She was pretty sure that he had never had to do anything like that in his life before and who knew? Maybe if they hadn't been stuck on an island where normal life had been temporarily suspended he would have called in people to pick up the slack so that he could remove himself from the thick of it, but they were on this island and he hadn't had a choice.

But he had risen to the occasion. Admirably.

She remembered something else, stuff they had talked about, and she was sure it wasn't her mind playing tricks on her. She had finally opened up about what her home life had really been like. Not given to personal confidences of that kind, it had been an enormous relief to let it all out. Growing up, not even her friends had known how much she had hated her father's mood swings, the sneering way he had of putting her down and putting her mother down, the atmosphere of tension that had been part and parcel of growing up. Her mother had maintained the front and a stiff upper lip and so, in the end, had she.

The last person she would ever have imagined talking to was Dio, yet she had, and she hadn't regretted opening up because he had proved to be a good listener.

And she'd been wrong. He hadn't used her. He'd said so. Her father had lied, had told her that Dio was a trumped up nobody who had married her for her social connections and her ability to fit in to the world he wanted to occupy—a world, her father had said, that was denied to him because he didn't come from the right background and didn't have the right accent.

She could have kicked herself for not really questioning that assumption. She should have known that Dio was so confident in himself, so much a born leader of the pack, that he wouldn't have cared less about any social pecking order.

But he'd hit the nail on the head when he had told her

that her father had known how to manipulate her own insecurities.

She'd been wrong about Dio.

Whatever his reasons for buying her father's company, and whatever bits and pieces of that awful conversation she had heard, she had misconstrued.

She'd had a lot of champagne and she had added up two and two and arrived at the wrong number and, because of that, they had had a sterile marriage in which all lines of communication had been lost. Indeed, she had ensured that those lines of communication had never been opened and he was far too proud a man to have initiated the sort of touchy-feely conversation he loathed.

He was proud, he was stubborn and…she was madly in love with him.

Her heart skipped a beat and she licked her lips, glad that she was alone in the room, because she would have felt horribly naked and vulnerable if he had been sitting in the chair, looking at her. Those amazing eyes of his saw everything.

She had fallen for him from the very first second she had laid eyes on him and she had papered over that reality with bitterness and resentment once they were married. She had told herself that he was just the sort of man she should have avoided at all costs; had told herself that the man for her was gentle, kind, thoughtful and considerate and that Dio was spectacularly none of those things.

How could he be when he had ruthlessly used her and married her for all the wrong reasons?

Now she felt as though the scales had been ripped from her eyes.

Not only had he proven just how considerate he could

be, just how thoughtful and caring, but he was no longer locked up in that box that she had turned her back on.

The divorce, which she had insisted on, was a mocking reminder of how stubbornly she had held on to her misconceptions and panic swept over her in a rush.

She'd hankered after a bright, shiny new life, free from someone who didn't give a damn about her, who had used her and who didn't care about whether she was happy or not.

But Dio…

She frowned.

Did he really care about her? She loved him. She knew that now. She had always loved him, which was why she had never been able to be in the same room as him without all her antennae being on red alert. She had fumed and raged but had still been so aware of him that her breathing became ragged whenever he was close to her.

But he had always been guarded around her and even here, making love, in the throes of passion, he had never—not once—let slip that he felt anything for her beyond lust.

She knew that she should take something from that, yet hope began to send out alarming little shoots.

Would he have been so solicitous if he didn't feel something for her?

Putting damp cloths on her forehead and cooking food, even if the food was usually the same fare of scrambled eggs and toast, counted for something…didn't it?

Alive to all sorts of possibilities, and feeling as right as rain, Lucy took herself off to have a shower. Then she slipped on the silk dressing gown hanging on the back of the door, making sure to leave her bra behind, and also making sure to wear some sexy lacy underwear, one of the few items of clothing she had brought with her.

She found him in the kitchen, some papers in one hand whilst with the other he stirred something in a frying pan. His back was to her and she took her time standing by the door, just looking at him.

She was seeing him in a whole new light. She had given herself permission to have feelings for this guy and now she appreciated the strength and beauty of his body, the muscular length of his legs, the powerful yet graceful arch of his back and the way his dark hair curled at the nape of his neck.

'I think you might be on the way to burning those eggs…'

Dio started and it took him a few seconds to register that Lucy was in the kitchen and looking so… So damned fresh-faced and sexy that it took his breath away.

She was in a dressing gown, loosely belted at the waist, flip flops on her feet, and she had draped her hair over to one side so that it fell in blonde, tumbled disarray over her shoulder.

No make-up. All one hundred per cent, natural woman.

His body clocked into a response that was fast, furious and immediate.

Just as it was, now, utterly inappropriate.

'What are you doing downstairs?' He salvaged the eggs. 'I was about to bring you your breakfast.'

Lucy strolled to the kitchen table and sat down. Here, as everywhere else in the villa, large windows allowed maximum light in and French doors led out to the lush back garden. It was already a warm, blue-skied day. The French doors had been flung open and a gentle, tropical breeze wafted in. She could smell the salty tang of the ocean air.

He was truly magnificent, she thought, in a pair of faded jeans and a white tee-shirt that did wondrous things for his physique.

'I woke up this morning feeling as right as rain.' She smiled and propped her chin in the palm of her hand. 'So I thought I'd come downstairs to have breakfast.'

'You should go back to bed,' Dio urged, abandoning the eggs to lean against the counter, arms folded.

'I know the doctor said that,' Lucy told him wryly, 'but I'm sure what he meant was that I could actually get out of it once I started feeling better...'

Dio gave her a long, considering look. She looked better. In fact, she looked in rude health, but was it an act? She had spent so much time apologising for her ill health getting in the way of why they were here that he wondered whether a sense of guilt hadn't propelled her into this act of sunshine and smiles.

'No need, Lucy.'

'No need for what?'

'Do you want breakfast? Of course you do. You need to eat.' Did he really want to get involved in a long, complex conversation? He'd already been knocked sideways by the last one.

And the last couple of days had thrown him off course even more. As marriages went, theirs had not been one that had involved any of the usual things he assumed were normally taken for granted. He had cooked meals—a first—and sat by her bedside, keenly aware that, whatever some doctor said, who knew whether this whirlwind virus would just miraculously disappear? He had mopped her brow and frankly put his own life on hold.

He'd barely managed to get any work done and his Hong Kong deal had been rearranged.

His life had always revolved around work so, like cooking meals, shoving it to the back burner had also been a first.

And she had told him things he had stupidly never suspected. How was it that it had never occurred to him that Robert Bishop, the man who had cold-bloodedly swindled his father, not to mention the people who had entrusted their pensions to him, might not have been the upstanding, loving family man he had assumed? If it walks like a duck, quacks like a duck and looks like a duck, then it was a duck. Robert Bishop had been a thoroughly unpleasant criminal, *ergo* he had been a thoroughly unpleasant man, full stop.

And Lucy…

So she might have got hold of the wrong end of the stick in one small detail, but if she only knew the half of it…

Yet his body was still on fire at the sight of her sitting there on the kitchen chair, looking as young and as fresh-faced as a teenager. The sun had brought out a scattering of freckles.

'Maybe we could have something aside from scrambled eggs…'

Dio forced a smile, while his mind continued to roam through all sorts of unexplored avenues. 'Are you telling me that you find fault with the chef?'

'Not at all. In fact, the patient couldn't be more grateful to the chef, although it has to be said that the chef's repertoire is very limited.'

'As you know only too well, I haven't made it my life's career to get to grips with a kitchen.'

'I'll help. Maybe we could cook something together. It'll do me good to be up and moving.'

Dio shrugged and Lucy stifled a sudden feeling of hurt but she stood up anyway and headed to the fridge, where she pulled out some ham, then she rifled through the cupboards and managed to locate enough ingredients for French toast.

'You sit, Dio. You've spent the past few days cooking for me; the least I could do is repay the favour.'

'Like you said, scrambled eggs don't exactly qualify as cooking.'

'I'll bet it's more than you've ever done.' She glanced over her shoulder and felt her heart constrict.

Had she disturbed whatever reading he had been doing? He couldn't have got much done while she had been ill and she knew that his Hong Kong trip had been postponed. He'd had to play the good Samaritan and she could hardly blame him if his mood wasn't all that great.

'You can prepare breakfast if you really want to, Lucy, but that's it. I'll get Enid in to take over the cooking arrangements for the remainder of the time that we're here. The last thing I need is for you to have a relapse.' This was what he had to do. Dio hadn't banked on long confessionals, and he hadn't banked on discovering what had really happened on their wedding night, what had led to her physical withdrawal from him. He got the uneasy feeling that something in her had changed towards him.

She had looked at him…differently after that little chat.

Maybe it was simply the fact that she'd been ill, running a high fever. Maybe that look in her eyes had been virus induced. Had she revised her rock bottom opinion of him because he had truthfully told her that he hadn't married her for her connections?

Did he want her to have revised opinions?

He recalled the way she had looked at him when they had been going out on their handful of dates. He had been charmed at the unexpected find of Robert Bishop's daughter.

Who'd have guessed…?

She had looked at him as though she were a starving waif and he were her specially prepared banquet.

He'd liked that too. What man wouldn't? He hadn't known just when it had occurred to him that she might play a part in the revenge plan that had been his companion for more years than he could remember. He didn't know whether that had been a conscious decision or not.

He just knew that emotions had never played a part in it for him. Emotions had never played a part for him in anything. He had absorbed one very simple reality growing up and that was that emotions were a train wreck waiting to happen.

Emotions had propelled his volatile, brilliant father into trusting a guy he considered a friend. It hadn't occurred to him to get signatures on a dotted line, to get lawyers involved when it came to his invention. He'd paid dearly for that oversight and they had all paid as well. Not just his father, but his mother, who had had to live with a bitter and disappointed husband and a son who had not been spared the details of a wrecked life.

No, Dio had learned from early on that emotions were not to be trusted. Logic, common sense, the intellect—those were the things to be trusted. They never let you down.

And money… With money came power and with power came freedom.

The only emotion Dio had allowed into his life was a healthy thirst for revenge and he had made enough money to ensure that, whatever form that revenge took, he would be able to cover it. His money had bought him the freedom to do just as he pleased when it came to ensuring that Robert Bishop paid for past sins.

He'd married Lucy because he'd fancied the hell out of her, because at thirty-two he'd been ready for marriage and the undeniable advantages it brought and because she'd been Robert Bishop's daughter—and how better to twist the knife than to parade her in front of her father as his wife?

But it would appear that nothing had been quite as it seemed.

He hadn't married a daddy's girl; he'd married someone who had been desperate to escape. For her the escape hadn't gone quite according to plan but, because she had been wrong about one small detail, did she now imagine that he was, in fact, the knight in shining armour she had originally placed all her trust in?

Because Dio didn't want that. Not at all…

She'd lost her virginity to him.

In the cold light of day, he was all too aware of the significance of that and it scared the hell out of him.

'I'm not going to relapse.' Lucy laughed uncertainly as she began focusing on food preparation.

'I've already had to postpone my Hong Kong deal… as you no doubt know.'

'Yes.' Tears stung the back of her eyes because he wasn't being cruel, he was just being honest. 'And I believe I apologised to you about being the cause of that.

Several times over. But I'm happy to tell you again that I'm sorry I screwed up all your precious plans.' Lucy said all of this in a rush without looking at him.

Dio raked his fingers through his hair and glared. He could tell from the slump of her shoulders that she was close to crying.

'I'm not asking for your apologies. I'm making sure that you don't overdo it and end back up in bed.'

'I know.' She clattered and began dipping the bread in the egg and frying. She could detect the grim impatience in his voice and it dawned on her that the honeymoon was well and truly over. 'Don't worry. I'll take extra care to make sure I'm bouncy and in top form and, if I do feel a little tired, I'll make sure I don't bore you by saying anything. These are done, although suddenly I'm not very hungry.' She was mortified at the foolish hope that had propelled her down the stairs in a dressing gown and not much else. Still not looking in his direction, she spun round with the frying pan in her hand to find that he had somehow, stealthily, managed to creep up on her.

He should have been at the kitchen table. Instead, he was an inch away from her and now he was gently removing the frying pan from her vice-like grip.

'I've never been a fan of crying women,' he murmured.

'And I've never been a fan of crying.' Lucy's voice wobbled. 'So you're in luck.'

Dio sifted his fingers through her hair and knew that he really shouldn't. She wanted out of the marriage and she would be a lot better off out. He was no knight in shining armour. He was, in fact, a lot worse than she had taken him to be.

What she needed—and he could see that, now that she had revealed her true colours—was a guy who could give her all those things she was looking for. Friendship, security of an emotional kind, a shoulder on which she could lean…

She needed one of those do-gooder, social worker types she had hitched up with at her out-of-hours teaching establishment. Her turbulent background had conditioned her for a guy whose ideal night in would be cooking together before settling down in front of the telly with just the dog between them. He didn't fit the bill, didn't want to and never would.

In which case, the kindest thing he could do would be to distance himself from her, starting from right now…

But when her hot little body was pressing up against him the way it was now, it was difficult to keep a handle on noble thoughts.

And she wasn't making things easy, either. She had pressed her face into his shoulder and he felt her body quiver as he stroked her hair with an unsteady hand.

Dio made a half-hearted attempt to create a little space between them and he wondered whether he was imagining that she held on to him just a little bit tighter.

'So you think I was being cruel when I reminded you of my deal in Hong Kong and the fact that I've had to reschedule it? You think I'm somehow blaming you?'

'I don't.' Her voice was muffled as she spoke into his shoulder. 'The only thing you really care about is work, isn't it?'

'How well you know me…'

A fortnight ago, had he said that, she would have shrugged and told herself acidly that that just about summed up why she didn't like the guy and never would—

forget about what he had done to her, forget about how he had used her.

Now that she knew that he hadn't used her, she was seeing him in a different light—seeing his humour, the depth of his intellect and the way he had looked after her when she had been ill.

There was a warmth there she'd never known existed. He might tell her that the only thing he cared about was work, but there was so much more to him than that, whether he accepted it or not.

She had sensed that all along, hadn't she? Which was why her heart had remained his even though her head had tried to persuade her otherwise.

If she let him, he would turn her away. She sensed that. Maybe she should fight for him. Would it be possible for her to seduce him into a place where he might find her presence indispensable to him?

They had slept together! Why shouldn't they carry on sleeping together? Why shouldn't this marriage become the real thing? She couldn't remember why she had been so passionate about getting a divorce.

They could stay as man and wife, but their lives would change in so many ways! She could carry on doing her maths classes at the centre…at the new and improved centre! Of course, she would have to come clean about who she was, but why should that be a problem?

She wriggled against him and the silky dressing gown dislodged just a tiny bit.

She made no attempt to belt it back into shape.

Dio groaned softly as her soft breasts squashed against his chest. When he looked down, he could see the shadow of her cleavage, the gentle swell of her naked breasts, nipples tantalisingly half-concealed by the dressing gown.

All he had to do was shift his hand, dip it under the silky fabric and he would be able to cup her breast, feel its weight in the palm of his hand…

'I want you to touch me,' she said huskily, shocking herself with her forwardness. She guided his hand under the dressing gown and felt his big body shudder. Heady satisfaction overwhelmed her. She was damp between her legs and she shifted, rubbing her thighs together and, more than anything else, wanting to feel his hand down there…

Even here, she'd shied away from making love in broad daylight, preferring to have the curtains drawn, which he had found very amusing.

Now, though…

She clasped his hand and stood back. 'This isn't the place.'

Dio knew that he could step in now and make clear his intention to put this honeymoon behind them…

Unfortunately, his body had other plans.

Maybe, if she'd said 'bedroom', he would have come to his senses. Maybe if she'd been predictable in her wants…

But she inclined her head to the kitchen window, tugged his hand and smiled shyly.

Dio followed the direction of her gaze and felt a charge of supersonic adrenaline flood through him.

'You like the curtains closed,' he said gruffly.

'Maybe I'm ready to branch out.'

'Luce…'

Lucy took a deep breath, untied the barely tied belt on the dressing gown and then shimmied out of it, leaving it to pool at her feet so that she was stark naked aside from her underwear.

She watched the flare of his nostrils, the way his eyes darkened, and noted the sharp intake of breath.

She'd never wanted him more desperately than she wanted him now. She'd spent months making sure to keep her heart under lock and key and, now that it had been released from captivity, she couldn't bear the thought of them walking away from one another.

She'd misjudged him and that put everything in a whole new light.

'I want to make love on the beach,' she said, brazening out her absolute terror of her body being exposed in the full, unforgiving glare of daylight. She was long and slim but her breasts had always been smaller than she'd wanted, her figure not voluptuous enough. She wondered whether he was making comparisons with all those other women he had slept with, now that he was actually seeing her like this, then she squashed that thought which did nothing for her self-esteem.

This is still honeymoon time… Dio thought, waving aside the introspection that had led him to resolve that he had to get out of a situation that had developed like a swift-moving hurricane. That the man he was definitely wasn't the one she thought she'd unearthed; that he had done what he had set out to do—he had acquired the company that should have rightly belonged to his father, had acquired Robert Bishop's daughter. Job done.

Now she was standing there, bare-breasted, her rosy-pink nipples pointing at him, her skin paler where it had been covered by her bikini top…her long slender legs going on for ever.

How was any red-blooded man to resist?

He walked slowly towards her and decided, in a sudden brainwave, that it would be downright callous to turn her away. She had a lot of issues. He'd never realised that before, but he knew now. She'd grown into adulthood with deep feelings of insecurity, unable to enjoy the looks she had been given.

If he rejected her now, all those insecurities would return tenfold.

Would he be happy being responsible for that? No. So…

In one easy movement, he pulled his tee-shirt over his head and smiled wolfishly as her eyes dipped compulsively to his washboard-hard stomach.

He never failed to get a kick at the way she looked at him, as if she was compelled to and yet, at the same time, was mortified to be caught doing it.

She was looking at him like that right now.

He linked his fingers through hers and gently brushed her hair away from her face.

'If you're sure…' Dio drawled.

'I am. Are you?'

At this moment in time, with an erection bulging against his trousers, Dio had never been more sure of anything in his life.

Outside the sun was already hot. The villa was set in its own very private grounds and the only sound they could hear was the sound of the sea lapping lazily on the shoreline.

A couple of days in bed had dimmed Lucy's recollection of just how stunning the tiny cove was: powder-white sand, sea so clear that you could see every polished stone you were treading on as you waded out, a distant horizon that was blue meeting blue.

The breeze felt wonderful on her naked breasts. She turned to him, laughing, holding her hand to her hair to keep it out of her face and, for just a few seconds, she was literally dazzled by his masculine beauty.

'Are you going to make me beg you to remove the rest of your underwear?' Dio's hand rested on the button of his jeans and he slowly pulled down the zip.

Lucy was riveted at the sight of him removing his jeans. The sun glinted over his bronzed body, exposing the flex of his muscles as he tossed the jeans behind him onto a rock, followed by his boxers.

Then, eyes not wavering for a second from her flushed, excited face, he touched himself and grinned.

'Okay. Your turn.'

Lucy slid out of her underwear, attempted nonchalantly to toss it to join his boxers, and then watched in dismay as a sudden gust of wind blew it into the sea.

Dio laughed and shielded his eyes from the glare. 'So…' He pulled her into him and she yielded without hesitation. His hard erection pressed against her belly made her quiver. 'Why the sudden sense of daring, my darling wife?' He nibbled her ear and she sighed softly and squirmed against him. 'What's happened to the shy little creature who wouldn't contemplate sex unless the curtains were tightly pulled?'

'Maybe you've kick-started a sense of adventure in me,' Lucy murmured and an unpleasant thought flashed through Dio's head like a depth charge…

Another man would be the recipient of her new found, so-called sense of adventure. He almost longed for the hesitant timidity that had made him keep those curtains tightly drawn.

His unexpected possessiveness was disturbing but thankfully short lived as he cupped her naked breasts in his big hands, teasing and thumbing the ripe swell of her nipples.

'Sand can be a nuisance,' he murmured, flicking his tongue against her ear, knowing just where she liked to be teased. 'So keep standing…'

He worked his way down until he was kneeling in front of her.

Lucy knew what he was going to do and her whole body thrummed with heady anticipation.

She loved it when he licked her down there. It had felt outrageously intimate the first time he had done it, and he had had to gently but firmly prise her legs apart so that he could settle between them, but having him tease her clitoris with his tongue was a mind-blowing experience.

She curled her fingers into his dark hair, arched back and parted her legs.

The sand was warm between her toes. She wanted to look down at his dark head moving between her legs but, on a soft moan, she closed her eyes and tilted her face up to the sun, losing herself in the wondrous sensation of the slow, inexorable build to her climax.

She cried out as she came against his mouth. Before she had time to return to planet Earth, he had hoisted her up, lifting her as easily as if she weighed nothing, and she wrapped her legs around him, feeling the thrust as he came in her.

No protection. And he was normally so careful. The realisation vanished as he pulsed inside her, driving her higher and higher until she was clinging, shuddering and coming in waves of intense pleasure, knowing that he was doing the same, feeling his release with an explosion of pure ecstasy.

Afterwards, they swam. Lucy would love to have been able to bottle the moment and treasure it for ever.

Failing that, as they returned to the beach towels he had brought down with him and lay on the sand, she wondered how she could engineer the conversation towards this very real thing that existed now between them.

Surely he must realise that things had changed?

They hadn't spoken about the divorce for days. She wondered whether her being ill had been a blessing in disguise. It had certainly been an eye opener for her. Had it been the same for him? So, he wasn't the kind of guy who was into long conversations about emotions, but that didn't mean that the emotions weren't there, did it?

She reached out and linked her fingers through his.

They were both gazing up, squinting at the bright blue sky through the fronds of the palm trees.

'So…' She allowed that one syllable to drag out tantalisingly.

'I should apologise.' Dio was down from his high and acknowledging that he had failed to take protection. He had known exactly what would happen out here, on the beach, and yet he had still failed to carry protection with him.

'Sorry?'

Furious with himself for overlooking something so vital, he stood up abruptly and strode towards the discarded clothing, slipping on his sandy boxers and jeans, which he brushed down.

Lucy immediately followed suit.

'I risked an unwanted pregnancy,' he said bluntly. 'I didn't use protection.'

Hearing him say those words, hearing the tone of his

voice, was like a slap in the face and she almost stumbled back.

'I'm sorry if I sound harsh.' He raked his fingers through his hair and cursed himself for not having had the will power to resist her when he'd known he should have. Instead, he had fabricated a bunch of non-excuses for enjoying himself one last time. Maybe if he hadn't discovered just how innocent she really was, maybe if she had been the hard-nosed opportunist he had always assumed her to be, he might have felt better about himself.

No, he *would* have felt better about himself. He would have taken what he had seen as his right and he would have walked away. As things stood, by exposing her own vulnerability, by revealing a softness he had never, ever expected, she had likewise exposed him for what he was: cold, ruthless, a man who had played the long game to get what he wanted.

They were poles apart. He was a shark to her minnow and he wondered whether he would have been quite so keen to secure her in his bid for revenge had he known. Probably not.

'I'm sure,' he began, heading back towards the villa, 'that, like me, the last thing you would want is to discover that you're pregnant. Especially…' he turned to face her fully '…when you consider that we're going to be getting a divorce.'

'It's okay,' she whispered. 'We were caught up in the passion of the moment. I'm sure it will be fine.'

Pain assaulted her on all fronts. She was giddy with it. How could he look at her like that, as though they hadn't just shared the most amazing experience ever? And it wasn't just about making love. It was so much more that they had shared. At least, that was how it was for her…

How could he be so...*callous*?

Desperation ploughed into her with the force of a sledgehammer and she hated it.

'How can you be like this, Dio?' The pleading whisper made her wince.

'Be like what?'

'We've just...made love...'

Dio could feel the unexplained horror of something breaking inside him and, far, far worse, the knowledge that it was inevitable that he was now walking down this road. 'It's what we came here to do. To make love. To have our honeymoon...'

'I know that!' Stripped of words, she stared at him, heart pounding so hard that it hurt.

'Then...what?' This was where revenge had finally taken him, to this impasse, to the only place he had ever reached before where he was powerless. He had thought his heart to have been wrapped in ice, immune to pain. He was discovering that it wasn't.

'What we had... Do you feel *nothing*?' Lucy longed to be cool, to just let it go, because she knew that she was trying to fight a battle that she was destined to lose, but the black void opening up at her feet seemed to galvanise her into a terrifying urge to cling.

Dio banked down the wave of unfamiliar emotion surging through him.

Her hands were balled into fists, her body rigid with accusation, and he recognised the searing hurt that lay behind that accusation; knew that from that angry hurt would eventually come the return of the cold dislike she had nurtured towards him.

And he knew that it was deserved. Hell, he knew that with as much certainty as he knew that night followed day.

'I feel we've had our honeymoon.' The words felt like shards of glass in his mouth but, deprived of any choice, he ploughed on, every muscle in his body braced for the job at hand—because that was what it was. 'And now we have to have our divorce…'

CHAPTER TEN

LUCY STOOD AND looked around the brand-new apartment which would now be her new home.

She knew that she should be feeling as pleased as punch. When she had finally garnered her courage all those weeks ago to bring up the matter of a divorce with Dio, this was exactly the sort of outcome she had had in mind.

No. This was a whole lot better than the outcome she had had in mind.

She had spent two weeks at the London house, during which time he had made sure to be abroad. He had fulfilled every single one of his promises, even though she knew, from what her lawyer had told her, that there had been no need because she had indeed signed up to a watertight pre-nup without even having realised it, idiot that she had been.

He had been generous beyond words. He had immediately arranged the purchase of the breath-taking apartment in which she now stood. It was in a prime location and there wasn't a stick of furniture she didn't like. Just as he had glimpsed the part of her that was the girl with the pony tail, the girl she really was, he had made sure that some member of staff chose items of furniture that were homely, comfortable and cosy.

She wasn't amazed that he had managed to acquire the perfect apartment so effortlessly.

Having spent a year and a half married to him, she knew that the one single thing money got when it came to purchase power was speed. What Dio wanted, Dio got. And what Dio had wanted had been this spectacular apartment.

What he had wanted was her out of his life, having got the honeymoon he had demanded when she had asked him for a divorce.

She sat on one of the boxes cluttering the living room and stared miserably out of the window. Her view, from here, was of the sky, a grey, leaden sky that seemed to reflect her mood.

She should be counting her blessings.

She was financially sorted for the rest of her life. The run-down building which had been her lifeline was in the process of a startling renovation which would make it the most desirable place in that part of London to which deprived children could go to further their education after school hours. She had no doubt that dozens would find their springboard to a better life. She had signed up to a teacher training course, something she had always wanted to do until marriage and Dio had swept her off her feet, and she would be able to do it without worrying about money. There were so many things for which she should be grateful.

And yet…

With a little sigh of pure misery, she strolled over to the window and stared down at the street below.

For a little window in time, out there in paradise, she had actually dared to hope. She had opened up to him, thankfully only stopping short of telling him how she felt about him—not that she was in any doubt that he didn't know—and she had dared to hope that destiny might veer off in a different direction.

She'd been such an idiot.

He might not have used her in the way she had been led to assume, but he hadn't cared about her either. Why had he married her? Probably because he had fancied her and had decided that she could be an asset to him. It had been a lazy decision and he hadn't banked on having a sexless marriage. Once sex had been put on the menu, he had been happy to grant her the divorce she wanted.

She knew that at least he had parted company caring enough about her to ensure her physical wellbeing, except what was the good of that when her emotional wellbeing was in pieces?

He had been ultra-courteous to her before they had parted company in London.

The sad truth was that she didn't want his bland concern. She wanted…

Frustrated with herself, she began unpacking. It was not yet ten in the morning and there was so much to do that she hardly knew where to begin. She had left most of her designer clothes behind but Dio had insisted she take the jewellery.

'It's worth a fortune, Dio,' she had protested half-heartedly and he had shrugged as they had boarded the plane.

'What do you suggest I do with it all?'

She had been tempted to tell him that he could always donate the lot to her replacement. *She* certainly had no intention of showing up to teach dripping in diamonds.

Now, she opened the first box of jewellery. It all belonged in a safe but instead she shut the lid and began placing the boxes at the back of the wardrobe, knowing that in due course she would have to do something more secure with them. Stick it all in a vault somewhere. Or maybe flog it all and donate the proceeds to charity. That seemed like a good idea.

She was so absorbed in her task, her thoughts so given over to silly, pointless rehashing over how her life had changed for ever, that she was barely aware of her entry phone ringing, at which point she wondered who it could be.

Maybe she half-expected it to be Dio but she was still shocked when she saw his grainy image on the little screen. He was glancing impatiently around him and then he stared up and she felt a quiver of nervous excitement invade her body.

'Are you going to let me in?' he asked tersely.

Lucy gathered her scattered senses to reply in a composed voice. 'What are you doing here?'

'I've come to…' *To what?* 'Just let me in, Luce. I need to talk to you.'

'Is it about the divorce? Because I thought it was all pretty straightforward.'

'I'm not enjoying this conversation on your entry phone.'

Lucy didn't think that she would enjoy a conversation face to face but she buzzed him in, knowing that he had probably come to check and make sure everything was okay with the apartment. He would be polite and concerned and she would want to scream with frustration.

'When did you get back?' she asked, as soon as she had opened the door to him. Her voice hitched in her throat. Never had he seemed so gloriously good-looking, his dark hair swept back, his lean, sexy face reminding her all too painfully of the intimate moments they had shared before his passion had given way to cool indifference.

'An hour and a half ago.' And he had had a struggle not coming sooner; had had to endure the slow, dawning realisation that he had made a terrible mistake.

He'd let her go. He'd allowed her to walk away and had then had to live with his uneasy conscience which would not let *him* go.

'And you came straight here?'

'I don't like putting things off.'

'Putting what off?' She had to tear her eyes away from his handsome face and was dismayed to find that she was perspiring, that her hands were shaking so that she stuck them behind her back before launching into a grateful speech about the apartment—about how wonderful it was, nervously laughing at the boxes still to be unpacked, offering him something to drink.

Dio glanced around him but he was driven to look at her. She looked scruffy. Her hair was tied back and she was in a pair of faded jeans, a baggy tee-shirt and some old, stained trainers. She couldn't have looked less like the polished beauty who had entertained clients as though she had been born to it.

But then, hadn't he already realised that that polished beauty was not her at all?

She also looked nervous as hell which, he thought wryly, could only be a patch on how nervous *he* was feeling. It was a sensation that was utterly alien to him. He knew that there was only one person in the world who could inspire that in him and that person was looking at him anxiously, as though half-waiting for some hidden hangman's noose to fall.

'Have you…had a period?'

'I beg your pardon?'

Dio raked his fingers through his hair and glowered. 'We made love without protection. Remember?'

'You've stepped off a plane and rushed over here to make sure I wasn't pregnant?'

Dio shrugged and frowned at her. He was hovering in the middle of the cluttered living room but now he sought out one of the chairs and sat down.

'I told you that it would be fine and it is,' Lucy said tersely, arms folded, as the reason for him descending on her became clear.

He hadn't come to make sure she had settled in all right. He had come to make sure there was to be no inconvenient situation to be dealt with. Woe betide her if he had dealt with one inconvenient situation only to find that another had come along! One that might be a little trickier to deal with!

'So you didn't have to dash over here in a flat-out panic thinking that there would be some other mess for you to try and clear up!'

'Why would I have panicked at the thought of you being pregnant?'

Lucy refused to give houseroom to anything stupid like hope. She'd been down that particular road already and look where it had got her. Nowhere.

His challenging remark was greeted with stony silence.

'Why don't you sit down?' Dio urged.

Likewise that was greeted with stony silence until

Lucy replied with simmering resentment, 'What for? You've told me why you came here and I've answered you. What more is there to talk about?'

'A lot, as it happens.' He hunkered forward, arms resting loosely on his thighs.

Lucy watched, bemused, as he slumped into silence. He was hesitant. Had she *ever* seen Dio hesitant? Even when she had asked him for a divorce, he had immediately and confidently responded with his demand for his denied honeymoon. He was the most self-assured person she had ever encountered in her entire life, yet right now…

'A lot…like what?' she asked, bewildered.

'I didn't marry you because of your background, Lucy.'

'I… I know that. I didn't at the time, but I know now. And you know I know.'

'But because I didn't marry you because of your background, doesn't mean that my intentions were entirely… honourable.'

'Dio, I have no idea what you're talking about.'

'It's a long story.' He sighed heavily and glanced at her with that same uncertainty in his pale eyes that filled her with apprehension. 'Your father wasn't entirely unknown to me when I decided to take over his company. In fact, I've known about your father for a very long time.'

'But how?'

'It goes back decades, Lucy. Before you were born. Our fathers knew one another.'

'I don't understand.'

'Skeletons in cupboards,' Dio said wearily. 'All families have them.'

'They do,' Lucy accepted, thinking of her own skeletons, no longer a secret from this man sitting across from her.

'Sometimes those skeletons have bones that rattle so much, they create all sorts of problems down the line. A long time ago, my father invented something pretty big and at the time he was friends with your father. They were at university together. My father was a boffin, yours was...what can I say? The life and soul of the party. I have no doubt that my father was somewhat in awe of your father's rich, playboy lifestyle. He was studious, poor, everything your father wasn't. When your father decided that he was worth investing in, my dad believed him. Unfortunately, his trust was somewhat misplaced.'

Comprehension was beginning to drip in and Lucy's eyes widened. 'My father...'

'Took everything. He took his family business and built it into something huge on the back of my father's hard work. I grew up with that and it... Let's put it this way, for a very long time I've been hell-bent on revenge. I waited my time, Lucy. I went to university and I made sure that I was better than good at everything I did. Fortunately, I seemed to have a knack for making money. I traded but quit that pretty quickly, just as soon as I had enough capital, along with a bank loan, to begin the business of acquisition. I made more money than I knew what to do with but there was only one thing I wanted to do with my millions and that was to wait until the time was right. I knew it would come because I knew what kind of man Robert Bishop was.'

'He was drinking himself into a hole...stealing from pensions.'

'He was and I knew just when to strike. The conversation you semi-overheard that night was when I told him exactly who I was.'

'He must have known before—he would have recognised your name.'

'Of course he did but the man was so arrogant, so sure that he was top dog, that it never occurred to him that he had become involved in a game in which there could only be one winner and that winner would be me.'

'So you went out with me…'

'I hadn't planned to. In fact, whilst I knew to the very last detail the progress of your father's company, I never had the slightest interest in the progress of his personal life. I didn't know you existed until I met you on that very first visit when I came to enquire about buying the company.'

'And my father encouraged us to go out…'

'I needed no encouragement, trust me on that, Luce. He knew who I was but he still stupidly thought that he could somehow con me into paying full whack for his company whilst keeping him on, honour intact. Maybe he thought he could use you as a bargaining tool to get an even better deal out of me. He'd swindled my father and he thought that we were cut from the same cloth. I have to admit that I didn't immediately disillusion him. I got involved with you and I was having…a good time.'

'You were having a good time…' Lucy said slowly, driven to search for an answer she knew she wouldn't want to hear. 'But did you plan on actually asking me to marry you?'

Dio looked at her steadily. He'd brokered hundreds of edge-of-cliff deals but never had he felt more nervous about the outcome of any situation…or more desperate to secure the outcome he wanted.

'No.'

'You planned on having some fun with me and then getting down to the main business of ruining my father as payback.'

'That's about the sum of it.'

'Why did you change your mind? Why did you decide to ask me to marry you?' Her puzzled, questioning eyes tangled with his steady, cool ones and it dawned on her that a man hell bent on revenge might find that revenge in all sorts of ways contrary to what he might have planned originally. 'I get it,' she said in a small, appalled voice. 'You figured that not only would you get the company but you would take me with it, and that way you would have wiped my father out on all fronts...'

Dio said nothing. He found it impossible to understand the whole business of revenge that had motivated him for such a long time, but then something so much bigger had come along and knocked him to the ground.

'How could you?' She sprang to her feet and paced the room, dodging the packing crates, her mind in turmoil, her stomach churning with his revelations.

With a flick of his hand he caught her as she jerkily paced past him and pulled her so that she toppled onto him, only to push herself back immediately, shaking with mortification and anger.

'I thought I'd misjudged you,' she flung at him bitterly. She clenched her fist because she wanted to slap his beautiful face so much that it was a physical pain.

'I know you did,' Dio told her gently. 'Just like I knew that finding out the truth would...hurt you. Why do you think I decided that the best outcome would be for me to walk away? Spare you the details?'

'Oh, how generous of you,' Lucy jeered with biting

sarcasm. She could feel the heat from his body against hers and the steady beat of his heart under her arm, which was pinned into position. He was only holding her lightly but she still couldn't move an inch. Tears stung the back of her eyes.

'Generous and, as it turns out, impossible,' Dio murmured. He could sense the effort she was making not to cry. He felt powerless to ease the pain and enraged that he was responsible for causing it, even though when all this began he had no idea that this was the route it would end up going down.

'Not impossible,' Lucy whispered. 'You could have just left me believing what I did.'

'You deserved to know the truth, Lucy, especially as…' He sighed, shook his head and released her abruptly.

Freed from his clasp, Lucy was dismayed to find that her body didn't immediately behave the way it should have. It took her a few seconds to leap away from him and sprint to one of the packing crates, where she sat, glaring at him.

'Especially as…*what*?' She wondered how many more revelations he had tucked up his sleeve.

'This isn't quite the end of what I have to say…'

'What more can there be, Dio? What more can you *possibly* have to say to me?'

'I thought I married you as a fitting way of making sure the wheel turned full circle. I took you for a daddy's girl and, yes, I thought that I could deprive him of more than just his company in one fell swoop. It never occurred to me that what I felt for you went far beyond anything to do with getting even with your father.'

'Oh, please…'

'I knew I fancied the hell out of you; I just didn't realise that I felt much more than that, which was why I was just so damned furious with myself when you decided that sleeping with me wasn't going to be on the table. I figured you'd strung me along to get me to sign on the dotted line, thinking, like your father, that I would be a sucker for your pretty face.'

Lucy flushed because, although that had been a horrible misunderstanding, she didn't emerge as flawless. They had both had issues with one another.

'I made sure I got what was mine, though… But I spared your father the humiliation of a prison sentence because of you.'

'Surely that would have been the ultimate revenge?'

'I found I couldn't do it.'

'Even when I refused to sleep with you?'

'Even then. Maybe…' he smiled wryly '… I wasn't quite as hard-nosed as I thought I was, or maybe I just fell in love with you and couldn't bring myself to take that ultimate step.'

'Fell in love with me?'

'It's why I lost interest in all other women the minute you came on the scene. The only woman I went to bed dreaming of was you. I thought that it was because I had never had the chance to take you to my bed. I thought it was a simple case of wanting what had been denied me…'

'Which was why you wanted the honeymoon, so that you could get me out of your system.' *He'd fallen in love with her?*

'I came here to tell you everything, Luce. I… I let you go, and I never should have done that, but I didn't know how to stop you, not when I knew that there was so much muddy water under the bridge.' He looked at her, wondered what was going on behind that beautiful, expressive face. If he lost her…

The thought filled his head like a blackness.

'When you say you *fell in love with me…*?'

'By that I mean I want you next to me for the rest of my life. I don't want a divorce, Lucy, although if you insist on one then I'll walk away. Unless,' he mused, 'I choose the other option of pursuing you relentlessly until you can't stand it any more and you just give in. I should warn you that I can go to great lengths to get what I want.'

Lucy threw him a wobbly smile. 'I can hardly believe what I'm hearing, Dio,' she confessed unsteadily. She sighed heavily. 'I fell in love with you the second you stepped into my life.' Her eyes flickered and got the response they wanted, the steady, tender gaze that warmed her to her very depths. 'It was like I was waking up for the first time in my life. I never thought…it never occurred to me that what was happening between us might not be real. I was so…inexperienced; when I overheard that conversation and then had it all confirmed by my father… You have no idea. It was like something inside me shrivelled up. I'd been bought, like something from a shop.'

'I was blind, Lucy. I hadn't been looking for love and I was arrogant enough to assume that it wouldn't find me unless I had been.'

'I was married to a guy I was crazy about but I was forced to tell myself otherwise. I knew that if I just confronted that truth I would break apart.'

'You played a part and I was responsible for that, my darling. You'd spent your life playing a part and then you were forced to continue…' And that hurt him. 'Little wonder that you were searching for an exit.'

'And I thought I'd found it. I could get back to what I had always dreamed of doing. I thought I'd be free, like a bird released from a cage, but then we went on our honeymoon and all the truths I'd shoved away out of sight began creeping out of their hiding places—and this time round I couldn't hide any of it from myself. I was still crazy about you. I'd never stopped…' Never had she felt more naked but that look on his face was still there, still warming her, taking her heart to heights she had never known existed.

'My darling…'

'I love you so much, Dio.'

'Revenge might not be an honourable emotion.' Dio stood up and walked across to her, dragging another packing crate so that their knees were touching. 'But I wouldn't have changed a second of those dishonourable emotions because they brought me to you, Lucy, and being with you is coming home. So…' He went down on one knee and looked at her with such tenderness that her heart melted. 'My darling almost-ex-wife, can I ask you not to divorce me?'

'I never thought I'd have a marriage proposal as weird as that!' Lucy's heart took flight and she reached forward and ran her fingers through his hair. 'So how can I say no? The past is behind us, all of it, and now…now we just have the future.' She laughed, leant to kiss him and lingered a bit more as their mouths met. 'My dearest husband for ever…'

* * * * *

Amanda Cinelli

Christmas at the Castello

'THERE'S STILL SOMETHING MISSING.'

Dara stood poised at the top of the staircase, looking over the Winter Wonderland theme that had transformed the opulent grand ballroom below her. Her assistant, Mia, waited patiently by her side. The younger woman had long ago got used to her boss's obsessive eye for detail. Devlin Events was about creating perfect Sicilian weddings for their high-profile clients. Over the past three years Dara had gained an army of the industry's most talented people and put them onto her payroll, but she still liked to oversee the final run-throughs at their most prominent venues. There was no one in the industry who could spot the little things better than she. And right now something was off.

Sweeping yet another glance around the room, she mentally checked off twenty-five tables, each adorned with a glittering crystal tree centrepiece. The overall effect was like a winter forest, with white and blue lighting completing the wintry theme. Her bride, a famous opera singer, had expressly forbidden any real flower arrangements on the tables. She had instead ordered hundreds of spherical arrangements of fresh white and pink roses, to be suspended from the ceiling in intricately symmetrical clusters.

Dara counted across the floating flower bombs—as

she had so lovingly named them. She got as far as the third row before she noticed the problem.

She sighed. 'They've doubled up on the colours.'

Mia's head snapped up. 'Are you sure?'

'Right over here.'

She walked down the marble staircase, the click of her heels echoing on the hard surface. She came to a stop underneath the offending decoration. It wasn't a major issue, but it was damned irritating now she'd noticed it. Mia's quiet voice came from behind her.

'Should I fetch one of the guys from the ceremony room?'

Dara shook her head. 'The wedding is due to start in two hours—the ceremony room is priority.' She smoothed down the front of her sleek red pencil skirt, trying to focus on everything *but* the mismatched flowers above her. Her eyes drifted upwards again.

Mia laughed. 'I'll go and get somebody.'

She disappeared out through the door, leaving Dara alone in the glittering winter ballroom.

The rest of the room was perfect. Her team was talented, and very capable of doing most of the work unchaperoned. She could pick and choose which events to attend, leaving her plenty of time to travel with her jet-setting husband. But it had been three weeks since she and Leo had been together—his newest business expansion into Asia had kept him away much longer than usual.

The restlessness that had plagued her over the past months seemed to have intensified in the absence of her husband. Three weeks was the longest they had spent apart. She was unable to shake the feeling that something was wrong—or perhaps something was about to *go* wrong.

Their joint venture into charity work in Sicily kept her busy. The Valente Foundation was doing fantastic work in some of the most disadvantaged areas on the island. And with Christmas fast approaching there was lots of volunteer work to do. But, as busy as she kept herself, something still kept her wide awake at night and staring at the ceiling.

Making a snap decision, she grabbed a ladder from nearby and set it up, removing her heels in the process. She didn't need to stand here waiting for a big strong man to fix the problem. There was no reason why she couldn't do it herself.

She quickly reached the top, keeping both hands in front of her on the cold metal for balance. It was true: if you wanted a job done well, sometimes you had to do it yourself. She focused on the arrangement, unhooking it from its place and lowering it down. It was heavier than she had expected, and she gasped as the world unexpectedly tilted on its axis.

'*Dio*, what *is* it with you and ladders?' a deep voice shouted from below her as the ladder suddenly righted itself and she was entirely vertical again.

'Leo.' Her heart gave a sharp thump.

Her husband was looking up at her, his hands holding the metal ladder steady. Dara dropped the flower arrangement and cursed.

'It's nice to see you still haven't lost your love of daring stunts, *carina*.'

Dara descended the ladder as quickly as she could manage and practically fell into her husband's arms. The familiar smell of him surrounded her, making her sigh involuntarily.

'Surprise…' he whispered huskily against her neck.

His permanent five o'clock shadow brushed against her skin and she shivered. Oh, how she had missed those shivers.

'You're a week early.' She pulled back in his arms.

He smirked. 'I like to be unpredictable.'

She loved it when he smiled like that, filled with mischief. Life was too serious without Leo around.

'I've got a surprise planned. Do you think you can manage a few days away from your work?'

'Right *now*? Leo, that sounds wonderful, but I'm needed here.'

Dara made a noise of protest, only to have him silence her with a finger against her lips.

'Do you remember your wedding vows, Signora Valente?'

Dara remembered their wedding day as if it had been yesterday. She had originally planned a simple ceremony on the beach in the Caribbean. But then they'd both realised there was only one place they could imagine becoming man and wife, attended by a few select family and friends: the *castello*, which had become the setting for the most romantic day of her life.

'We both agreed to remove that medieval part about obeying one's husband from our vows.' She raised a brow.

'I'm talking about the part where we promised to spend each and every day loving each other.' His gaze darkened as his hand drifted lower on her back. 'And it seems I've got about twenty-two days of loving to make up for.'

His mouth lowered to hers and captured it in a scorching kiss full of dark, sensual promise.

A muted cough interrupted them from their interlude. Mia, accompanied by one of the movers, stood awkwardly at the top of the stairs. Dara stood back from their sensual embrace, her cheeks flaming.

'Nice to see you home safe, Mr Valente,' Mia said and blushed. 'Shall I book you both into the restaurant for lunch?'

'I've come to steal my wife away, I'm afraid.'

Dara placed a hand against her chest, straightening her blazer as casually as she could manage under the scrutiny of her staff. 'Leo, I can't just leave two hours before an event—'

'Actually, you can,' Mia interrupted, blushing even more as both Leo and Dara turned to face her. 'What I mean is, Dara, you've been working so hard… What's the point in being the boss if you can't take some time off? The rest of the team can see this through perfectly well.'

Leo moved forward, grabbing Dara's shoes from the floor. 'Mia, you are the voice of reason.'

Dara shook her head, smiling. 'This is crazy. I have a million things I should be doing.'

'That's what makes stealing you away so much fun.' He winked, pulling her by the hand. 'Mia, you are only to call my wife if there is a fire or some other catastrophic event.'

'Understood, sir.' The assistant saluted, giggling uncontrollably as Leo commandeered his speechless wife from the room in her bare feet.

'Is the blindfold really necessary?' Dara asked, feeling for Leo's hand in the close confines of his sleek sports car.

'Necessary? Perhaps not,' Leo's voice purred silkily somewhere next to her ear. 'But it adds to my enjoyment.'

Dara reached out, her hand coming into contact with his arm: a band of hard muscle covered in the rich silk of his dark shirt. 'Well, in two years of marriage you've never mentioned this particular fantasy.'

Dara's breath whooshed out of her lungs as a warm hand settled possessively upon her inner thigh. It had been weeks since she'd felt her husband's hands on her body, and the sensation was just as addictive as she remembered.

'I've never been one for power plays, but I must say I am enjoying the effect so far,' he murmured seductively.

'I'm open to the blindfold, but I'm drawing the line at handcuffs,' she replied, focusing on the agonising slowness of his fingers as they progressed towards the hem of her skirt.

'We're hot enough in the bedroom without adding props, *carina*,' he rasped, gripping her thigh and squeezing gently. 'And I'm liable to stop this car on the side of the road if you don't stop making those delicious little noises.'

Dara smiled to herself, hearing his laboured breathing. 'I'll behave myself if it means avoiding an accident. Still, I'm not opposed to you being so out of control.'

He chuckled. 'I'll make note of that.'

Less than fifteen minutes later the car had moved off the motorway and onto rougher terrain. She had expected him to take her to the private airfield where they normally housed the jet, but he wouldn't have needed to blindfold her for that. The past Christmases of their relationship had been spent travelling abroad. Sipping champagne at the top of the Eiffel Tower…exploring deserted beaches in Bali. She wondered what on earth he had planned this year. Curiosity made her stomach jolt with excitement as she felt the car suddenly pull to a smooth stop.

Leo jumped out from the car, ordering her to wait as

he opened her door and helped her out into the crisp night air. He gently removed the blindfold, allowing Dara a moment as her eyes adjusted to her surroundings.

She looked up at the familiar facade of Castello Bellamo and felt her breath catch. Thousands of tiny twinkling fairy lights adorned the steps to the double doors. The entrance glowed as though lit up by some kind of magical force.

'The real surprise is inside.' Leo took her by the hand and led her up the steps and through the open doors into the grand hallway.

The *castello* had always been a magical place to her, with its vaulted ceilings and mysterious corridors. But now it simply took her breath away. Thick garlands of flowers adorned each side of the staircase, and tiny ornamental elves sat on a side table surrounded by candlelight. The light from the chandelier above had been left dimmed for maximum effect, and she could see a warm glow emanating from the doorway leading into the front sitting room.

'Leo, the place looks like something from a fairy tale.' She sighed, wandering through the archway. Her breath caught as she took in the enormous Christmas tree that dominated the room. The tree had to be at least nine feet tall, and was perfectly decorated in an array of red and gold. 'Did you do this all by yourself?' she asked, still stunned by all the effort he'd gone to.

'I had some help,' he admitted. 'I remembered you spoke about how much you loved the traditional family Christmases you had as a child.' Moving his weight onto one foot, he leaned against the archway and watched her. 'Do you like it?'

Dara turned to him, feeling tears well up in her eyes

as she realised that her powerful jet-setting husband was actually nervous.

'Leo, this is so thoughtful, I'm actually—' She swallowed down her emotion, trying not to ruin the moment with silly tears.

'What's wrong? Have I upset you?' Leo was by her side in an instant and enveloping her into his strong embrace. 'I know that we usually spend this time of year somewhere warmer and more exotic. Are you disappointed?'

Dara shook her head quickly, looking up into the brilliant emerald depths of his eyes. He was so serious, so concerned, and yet she couldn't seem to find the words to assure him that this was wonderful.

'It's perfect,' she rasped. 'Thank you.'

She felt his arms relax around her, pulling her closer into the wall of his chest. She tilted her head up and claimed his mouth in a kiss full of heat and promise.

Leo groaned and smoothed his hands down Dara's back slowly, allowing his hands to rest on her supple curves. She was still as addictive as ever, his wife. And he'd be damned, but he couldn't wait another moment before having her.

The soft rug before the fire made for an excellent makeshift bed. He lowered them both to the floor slowly, unbuttoning his shirt in the process. Dara began to pull at the buttons on her own blouse, but Leo had other plans. He laid a hand gently on top of hers.

'I've been fantasizing for weeks about undressing you,' he whispered sensuously as he ran a slow, torturous hand down her ribcage.

Dara shivered, heat rising in her cheeks. 'You still fantasize about me?' She looked doubtful.

'*Amore mio*, you are the only woman who gets me like this. Look at me—I'm rock-hard and struggling for breath after one kiss.'

Dara's eyes sparked with possession as she laid her hand on his belt buckle. 'I'm glad. Because I plan on being the only woman for a long time yet.'

Leo sucked in a breath as her fingers undid the buckle, lowering the zip of his trousers in one smooth movement. Her hand wandered, momentarily grazing his erection and making him groan.

'Such a tease,' he growled, pushing her back down onto the rug. 'This is *my* fantasy, remember?'

Leo grabbed the waistline of her pencil skirt, tugging it low on her hips before removing it completely. What he saw beneath made his eyes widen and his heart thump uncomfortably. Delicate thigh-high stockings covered her legs, held in place by a black lace garter belt.

'This is new.' He felt his throat run dry.

Dara's blush deepened. 'I had a feeling you'd like it.'

Leo ran his hand across the flimsy lace, feeling the heat of her skin underneath. A matching thong was the only thing that lay between his fingers and the moist heat of her delicate skin beneath.

'I planned to take my time…' He bit his lower lip, watching her eyes darken as she arched her hips against his hand. He leaned down, taking the lace between his teeth as he undid one catch and rolled the stocking slowly down the smooth skin of her thigh. Discarding it on the floor, he turned his attention to the other thigh and repeated the action. Dara shivered, unconsciously spreading her thighs wide for him. Or maybe it wasn't unconscious at all; maybe she was deliberately trying to drive him insane.

Pushing the thin lace to one side, Leo trailed one fingertip along the slick crease between her thighs. Dara moaned under his touch, pressing closer into his hand. He could tell that she was ready for him. But a wicked part of him made her wait a moment longer. He leaned just close enough to blow a single breath of hot air against her sensitive flesh.

Dara gasped, gripping the hair at the nape of his neck to pull him closer.

The action drove him wild. She was flushed and breathing harshly. Leo obeyed her breathless plea, pressing his lips to her tender flesh and hearing her groan in response. He moved his mouth in sync with his fingers, driving her closer and closer to that point of no return. He felt her body tense under the onslaught of pleasure. A single curse escaped those delicate lips as she reached her climax.

No sooner had her aftershocks subsided than he was thrusting deep inside her, sinking into her molten heat with a muttered curse of his own. 'Oh, *Dio*, I've missed this.' He groaned as he built up a steady rhythm, spreading her legs wide as he leaned down and took one taut nipple into his mouth.

Dara caressed his back with her fingertips as he drove into her with all the control he could muster.

His release came hard and fast, taking them both by surprise.

Once the wave of pleasure had subsided, he sank down on the rug by her side and exhaled hard.

Dara sat up on one elbow, tracing the hairs on his chest idly. 'That was worth the wait.'

Leo murmured his agreement, feeling her hands on his chest and listening to her rhythmic breathing as his eyes closed.

Dara couldn't sleep. She stared up at the two stockings that hung over the fireplace. They looked so plain, so small on that huge mantelpiece. That same feeling that had plagued her for the past few months threatened to overcome her again.

This wasn't about the stockings.

The same way as her frequent trips to Syracuse had nothing at all to do with business.

Since they had opened up their charitable project, the Valente Foundation, she had been required to attend a handful of fundraisers and benefits. Her presence wasn't necessarily required in any of the institutions they supported on a day-to-day basis, and yet she had found herself taking on the role of patroness at the Syracuse orphanage with the aim of being a silent figure.

The first couple of trips had been to check on the progress of some renovations, and then she had arranged for a new playground to be built. That playground had been finished in the summer, and yet she still found reason to visit as often as she could manage. With Leo away she had found herself making the hour-long trip up to three times a week. Even the ever-smiling house matron had begun to look confused at her continued presence.

There were stockings up on the fireplace at the orphanage too. Seventeen of them, side by side, hanging on a string in the common room. Now that Leo was home she supposed she would find no reason to go to Syracuse again. He would ask questions about why she visited only one orphanage—why not all the others? Why not the hospitals? He would know, just as she knew, that her actions weren't about being charitable at all.

The press had been merciless in the beginning: everyone had wanted to see Leo Valente transformed from playboy to father. Dara had never made a secret of her inability to bear children, so it had been no surprise that the press had caught wind of it soon after their wedding. The rumour mill had gone into overdrive. Would they adopt? Would they use a surrogate? They'd been a hot topic for quite some time.

They had decided that their business was their own, and that their choice to remain childless was both private and definite.

Hot tears threatened to fall from her eyes now, as emotion built in her throat. It just didn't make sense. She had made it clear from the start—before they married—that children were not in her future. She'd made her peace with that on a hospital bed, upon being informed that her condition was incurable. She hadn't been foolish enough to hold out any hope of some day carrying a child of her own. It was better to be realistic. She had never had strong maternal tendencies anyway. For goodness' sake, she was a workaholic and a complete neat freak—both qualities didn't exactly mix well with motherhood.

She knew all this and yet she had been selfish enough to go back to the orphanage after that first time. Selfish and inconsiderate.

She had been plagued by a sense of restlessness these past few months. Married life was wonderful, and her success in her career was at an all-time high. And yet it seemed as if the only time she felt whole these days was when she was there.

The children were wonderfully well behaved, thanks

to the efforts of the brilliant schoolteachers led by Matron Anna. Each visit brought with it new adventures filled with laughter. Life was less serious, less stressful.

A vision of small brown eyes and a playful grin filled her mind. A small hand holding on to hers so tightly. She couldn't keep lying to herself. There was only one reason why she kept going back there, and that reason had a mischievous smile and liked to curl up on her lap to read.

She heard the sounds of Leo waking up behind her and tried to wipe away the tears from her cheeks without him noticing. Tried and failed.

'Dara?' He was up in an instant, sleep clouding his eyes. 'Has something happened?'

'I'm fine—let's just go up to bed.' She shook off his embrace, pulling a blanket from the sofa to drape around her shoulders.

'You've been crying.'

'I'm fine...honestly.' She tried to avoid his penetrating gaze, turning to poke at the dwindling embers in the grate.

'You've been acting strangely since we got here. I thought you loved this place—I thought being here on a more permanent basis would make you happy.'

'It does. I'm looking forward to us spending Christmas here together.'

'Dara, I don't know what is going on with you. You've been avoiding some of my phone calls while I was away. Even when I specifically called when I knew you'd be finished with work. And today my driver mentioned that you've been disappearing by yourself for hours at a time. With no reasonable explanation—'

'You had your driver keeping tabs on me?' Dara was incredulous.

'I wasn't going to pay it any attention, because I trust you. But dammit, Dara, you're hiding something from me and I want to know what it is. *Now.*'

'What do you think? That I'm cheating on you?'

Leo crossed his arms, looking darkly into the glowing fire. 'I'd like to think I know you better than that.'

Dara placed her hands on her hips. 'Well, it sounds like you're accusing me of something. I'm entitled to *some* level of privacy. Just because we're married, it doesn't mean we need to live in each other's pockets, for goodness' sake.'

She moved to walk away and felt his hand move gently to her wrist.

'Dara…'

His voice was quiet, and something in its tone appealed to her logic. She knew she was behaving out of character. And that he must be concerned. He had flown for almost twenty-four hours to come here and surprise her, and here she was shouting at him for asking if she was okay.

The realisation brought even more tears.

'I'm sorry.'

She sat down heavily on the sofa, hiding her face in her hands. She felt him come to her, felt his solid warmth slide alongside her and envelop her as she sat there trying to make sense of why she was falling apart.

'I've been going to the orphanage in Syracuse,' she admitted. 'It started as a simple project to update their facilities. But then it became…more.'

Leo sat silently, watching her reveal her secrets.

'I was there one day, helping to choose wallpaper for the common room, when one of the smallest children—

a boy—walked right up to me and grabbed my hand. The other children had avoided me on previous visits; I was a stranger with a foreign accent and a fancy suit. I was unapproachable.' She smiled to herself. 'But not him. He grabbed on to my hand and asked me to come and see his drawings. He had drawn a picture of a house by the sea. He gave it to me as a gift and asked me if I would come back again. So I did.'

Leo remained silent for a moment, watching her. 'Why do you feel the need to hide all this? It's charitable work.'

'Don't you see? It's *not* work to me. I *want* to be there. It makes me happy to be there with all the children. But most of all with Luca…'

'Luca is the boy's name?' Leo asked quietly.

Dara nodded. 'It's unfair of me to grow attached. Because he's just a child and he will think that I want to… that we might want to…' The words stuck in her throat, unable to come out.

'That you might want to become his mother?' Leo said.

Dara looked at him quickly, as though he had struck her. That one word was enough to make her mind turn to panic.

Mother.

'I won't go back again. I suppose I'm only just realizing that I've used the orphanage to relieve my restlessness. To occupy myself.'

She stood up and walked to the Christmas tree, touching one of the golden baubles and making it spin.

'It was a selfish act and I'm feeling guilty, that's all.'

Dara turned back to her husband. He sat completely nude on the sofa, watching her with a look so concerned it melted her heart. If she told him any more she would only regret it in the morning. It wasn't that she feared his judgement. In fact it was completely the opposite. She feared his pity.

Leo had taken the news of her infertility in his stride from the moment she'd revealed her secret to him. He had been understanding, and he had helped her to realize that her condition did not define her.

To bring up all those old insecurities now would only belittle how far they had come as a couple.

That was the thing, though—she wasn't quite so confident that she had ever rid herself of them at all. Rather, she had just chosen to focus on being the beautiful woman that Leo made her feel she was and ignored the sad and broken woman of her past.

She bit her lip. Leo was looking at her intensely, waiting for her to speak. She couldn't tell him the truth, not tonight anyway.

'I'm sorry. I feel like I've ruined this wonderful night with my own silly ramblings.' She shook her head, banishing the dark thoughts from her mind.

She walked to him and straddled his lap.

'Dara, we're having quite a serious conversation here, and I will find it very difficult to concentrate with you in this position.'

He shifted, but she moulded her body even closer to him.

'I've had enough talking for tonight.' She leaned over him, nipping his earlobe just hard enough to make him groan. 'You said we have twenty-two days to make up for, and I plan on obeying my husband's wishes.'

She smiled wickedly, banishing all other thoughts from their minds as their bodies instinctively moved against each other.

Leo sat on the terrace, looking out at the midday winter sun shining on the choppy waves of the bay. Most of their morning had been spent in bed, making up for lost time. But some time after brunch Dara had found herself taking a call from Mia about something vitally important. Rather than being annoyed at the interruption, Leo had once again been impressed at how much his wife's company relied on her.

She ran Devlin Events like a well-oiled machine—just as he would expect. But still her staff looked to her for guidance, and felt comfortable in doing so. This was one of the main reasons for her skyrocketing success. Her employees were satisfied, and therefore so were her clients. Add that to the fact that she was unbelievably talented and passionate, and it could only be a recipe for success.

He watched her through the terrace doors as she booted up her tablet computer and wielded it like a clipboard. She was tense, even after a night of being thoroughly made love to.

Her revelation about her trips to the orphanage had confused him. Dara had never shown any interest in children. He had never even seen her speak to a child, not to mention drive out of her way to go and visit one. But recently he had begun to feel a distance between them. They both had busy careers, but they usually made sure to keep time for each other.

Leo stood, suddenly needing to walk. He took the path down along the cliff-face—the same path he'd used to take as a boy. He stopped on the flight of steps that led down to the old boathouse, remembering his childhood self rushing down the stone steps, furiously trying to hold in the tears and escape his nightmarish life. Living with a mentally ill mother had forced him to live in silence. His formative years had been spent in isolation, and in fear of upsetting her with his mere presence.

Those memories no longer held the same dark power over him—not since Dara had come into his life. Now every time he walked down here he was reminded that he was happier than either of his parents had ever been.

Right now, he was impressed that the little boathouse was still standing. He pushed the door open with a creak and ducked his head inside.

A row of plastic boxes lined the floor—he had insulated the place last year, once they had decided to use it for storage rather than leave it to rot. Flipping the lid of the box nearest the window, Leo idly surveyed the contents. A collection of coloured yo-yos lay inside, once his favourite boyhood hobby. He picked up a red one and spun the yarn tightly between the circular wooden discs.

He had spent many days inside these four walls, practising his skills and hoping for someone to show them to. He held the yo-yo tight in his hand before letting it fall to the ground and bouncing it back up easily. His tricks had been numerous, all learned from a book he had got as a gift from his father. He knew now that his father's secretary had probably chosen it, but at the time he had taken it as a challenge to impress the old man. And, as he did with most tasks, he'd poured his heart and soul into it.

In a way he was no different from the little boy who had captured his wife's attention. Leo might not have been an orphan, but he knew what it meant to crave a connection. He had that with Dara now—he felt the completeness that came from the love of a good woman. He had poured all his efforts into creating a life together with his beautiful wife.

Since meeting Dara he had slowly lost interest in the party scene—except for when he opened up a new club. As a bachelor, he had spent his leisure time mainly involved in drinking too much and buying the fastest cars. He'd had no difficulty living in hotels for months at a time. He hadn't known what it meant to have a home.

Dara had shown him just how fulfilling life could be. But now he got the feeling that she felt their life was lacking somehow. If she was happy, why was she escaping to Syracuse every chance she could get?

An image of the longing in her eyes when she spoke about the child there filled his mind. It was suddenly blindingly clear that Dara had developed a newfound yearning for motherhood. And somehow that yearning wasn't something she felt comfortable sharing with him. The thought jarred him, leaving an uncomfortable knot in his stomach.

Leo ran a hand through his hair and threw the yo-yo back into the box. He had never once questioned Dara's steadfast opinion on family. She had made it clear that she would never have children, and that had suited them both. The idea of fatherhood had never been something he aspired to. His own father had been a spectre in his life—one who had drifted in and out, leaving him uncertain and confused. As an adult he had never once considered the idea of starting a family of his own.

But lately he had begun to grow tired of the constant

travelling. These days the only place he wanted to be was here, with his wife, in their true home. He had wanted to say that to her last night, but they had got sidetracked.

He walked back to the *castello* just as evening was setting in and found Dara waiting for him in the kitchen. A bottle of vintage Prosecco sat on the table, two glasses beside it.

'I'm sorry I took so long.' She winced, pouring him a generous glass of wine.

Leo took a sip, appreciating the taste for a moment before shrugging. 'You have a business to run, *carina.* I have to accept that I can never have you all to myself.'

'I've turned my phone off for the evening, so I am one hundred per cent yours. No distractions.' She smiled, pressing her mouth to his.

Leo held her at arm's length, noticing the shadows under her eyes. 'Good. Because I'd like to continue our discussion from last night.'

Dara removed herself from his arms, turning to take a long gulp from her own glass. 'I'd rather we just leave that, actually. I must have been overtired and emotional.'

Her laugh didn't fool him. 'Dara, are you unhappy?' he asked, and watched her face snap up with alarm.

'Why on earth would you think that?'

'You seem...unfulfilled, somehow. These trips to Syracuse tell me that perhaps you might have changed your mind about some things.'

Dara looked momentarily miserable, her expression filled with intense sadness before shifting back to a mask of calm. Anyone else might not have noticed, but Leo knew her better than anyone.

'It's nothing that I plan to act on,' she said coldly. 'There's no need for you to worry.'

'Why would I worry? We are husband and wife, Dara. We make these kinds of choices together. Maybe I should go with you to Syracuse so you can help me to understand.'

'That's definitely *not* what I want,' Dara snapped.

'Per l'amore di Dio.' Leo sucked in a breath to control his frustration. 'Dara, for God's sake, what *do* you want?' he shouted harshly, feeling instant remorse as she flinched.

They stood in silence for a moment, toe to toe in the silence of the kitchen.

'I won't be shouted at.' Dara spoke quietly. 'I need some time alone. I'll see you at dinner.'

She practically ran from the room. Ran away from him.

Leo frowned, looking out of the window at the waves crashing against the cliffs. He had lost his temper—but could she blame him? He was her *husband*, and yet she was determined to battle whatever was bothering her alone. He had a right to know what this was about.

Clearly the answer lay in Syracuse. If she wouldn't go with him, then he would have to go alone.

Dara awoke to a note on her pillow from Leo, telling her that he had some business to attend to and that he would return by the afternoon. His words were plain and to the point, with none of the flowery terms of affection that they usually used. She felt a pang of hurt that he hadn't woken her before leaving, and now she faced a day in the *castello* alone with her thoughts.

She had been hostile and unfair last night. And now she had driven a wedge between them. She sighed, falling back onto the soft Egyptian cotton bedspread, and stared up at the ceiling.

It wasn't that she didn't *want* to share her inner turmoil with her husband. She just felt that it was pointless to do so. Yes, she had formed a bond with Luca. Yes, for the first time in her life she had felt the all-encompassing yearning to care for a child as her own. But she would never do it. She would never be so naive as to assume that she was in any way qualified to be a parent. She was a very good wedding planner, and she hoped she was a satisfying wife. But she was not cut out to be somebody's mother.

Her own mother had been warm and caring. She had given up her career in hotel management to stay at home as a full-time parent and had made it clear that she believed all women should do the same. Dara knew that Leo didn't think that way—he went out of his way to promote equality in his company, and often commented on how proud he was of his wife's accomplishments. And yet the image of her mother baking in the kitchen would always be her measure of what a good wife looked like.

She stared out at the waves crashing onto the cliffs below. Why was she having all these thoughts now? She *loved* her life. She had more than most women could dream of.

Needing to escape her overactive thoughts, she walked to the window. The winds were too high today to walk down on the beach, and being outside in the chilly December air wasn't her idea of a relaxing getaway.

It had been Leo's idea to take time off work, and yet

here he was abandoning her on their third day. Clearly he was annoyed, and was choosing to punish her.

Her mind wandered back to the orphanage once more. She was restless and annoyed with herself for allowing this charade to go on for so long. It wasn't fair to the little boy or to the hopeful orphanage staff. She needed to explain herself and give them a clear idea that she would no longer be visiting.

She could see Luca one last time.

Before she'd even realized what she was doing, she'd picked up her car keys and was powering up the cobbled driveway in her Porsche. She could be at the orphanage within the hour, and back well before lunchtime. Leo wouldn't even know she'd gone anywhere.

The familiar white stucco facade of the orphanage was like a balm to the uncomfortable ache in her chest. Dara knocked on the door and stepped back when it swung open to reveal the kind-faced head of the orphanage—Matron Anna.

'Signora Valente, I'm surprised to see you here.' She frowned. 'I thought you were in Palermo this week?'

'What would make you think that?' Dara smiled as she stepped inside and let the younger woman take her jacket.

'Signor Valente said that you were so busy this week…'

'He did? When were you speaking with him?' Dara frowned, just as a roar of laughter came from the nearby common room. A familiar voice drifted down the hallway—a deep male voice filled with mischief and laughter.

Dara moved silently towards the doorway of the common room, her heart hammering uncomfortably in her chest. The children were all gathered in the centre of the room, on the floor, and each of their little faces was beaming up at the man who stood in the centre of their circle. Leo stood poised with a red yo-yo in his hand. His posture was like that of a magician about to wow his crowd.

'And now for my next trick…' he proclaimed, waiting a moment as the children shouted loudly for him to continue. 'This one is called the lindy loop. Are you ready?'

The excitement in the air was palpable, and every eye in the room was trained on Leo as he set the red object on an intricate movement up in the air. The yo-yo caught several times on its string, before spinning up into the air and down to the ground and then landing safely back into its master's hand.

The children clapped loudly, shouting multiple requests for new tricks at their entertainer. Leo was calm and indulgent, chatting easily to the crowd of little people in a way Dara had never seemed to master. She had spent weeks trying to gain the confidence of these kids, and the most she'd managed had been sharing lunch at the same table.

Luca always stayed by her side, though.

Her thoughts back on the present moment, she suddenly absorbed the fact that her husband was *here*. In the orphanage. He had lied to her, and for that she should be furious.

And yet all she felt was a same sense of anticipation. As if she was hurtling head first down a hill and she had no power to stop it.

As she watched, Luca stepped forward from the crowd

of children. His soft black curls were falling forward into his eyes as they always did. He had the kind of unruly hair that refused to behave under the ministrations of any brush. She imagined Leo's hair would be much the same if he let it grow any longer.

Catching her thoughts, she shook her head and watched as her husband sank down to his knees to listen to the young boy whisper something into his ear. Leo listened intently for a moment, before breaking into a huge grin. Luca smiled up at him and they both laughed together at their secret joke.

And Dara felt her heart break completely.

Turning from the door, she walked quickly down the corridor and out to her car. The drive home passed in a blur. Her body felt numb and her insides shook violently.

Once she reached the familiar facade of the *castello*, she walked to the stone wall that overlooked the famous cliffs of Monterocca. And only then did she let the tears come. Great racking sobs escaped her throat and sent violent tremors through her.

It was unthinkably cruel that Leo should look so perfect surrounded by children. The one thing that she could never give him. She wept for the children she would never bear. The children she had denied wanting for so long.

Soon the sound of tyres squealing down the driveway interrupted her silence. Heavy steps were moving fast across the courtyard towards her.

Dara turned just as Leo came to a stop. 'Where have you been?' she asked innocently.

'You know where,' Leo gritted. 'They told me that you arrived and then left—driving like a mad woman.'

'You lied to me,' Dara said, her voice almost a whisper.

'I needed to understand.' He stood with his arms crossed.

'And *do* you? Do you understand now why it was so selfish of me to get so attached?'

'To tell the truth, Dara, no—I don't.' He sighed. 'You keep saying you've been selfish. But I don't understand how you can consider giving your time and attention to those children as selfishness.'

'I wasn't *giving* anything, Leo. I was taking. I got too close. I let Luca get attached to me because it made me feel…needed.' She took a deep shuddering breath, shaking her head at her own foolishness. 'It made me feel like—like I was his mother.' She bit her lip. 'Can't you see how wrong that is? I've given him hope for something that can never happen.'

'What makes you believe that it can never happen, Dara?'

'Look at me, for goodness' sake. I'm a control freak who works crazy hours and spends half the year travelling around the world with my nightclub magnate former playboy husband.'

'That's…quite a mouthful.' Leo's brows rose.

'It's the truth.' She shrugged. 'We're not family people. Aside from the fact that we can never have our own biological children.'

Leo walked past her to the ancient stone boundary wall, leaning over to peer down at the rough sea below them. 'I might be a jet-setting former playboy, but I think I would be ten times the father that mine was.'

Dara froze. 'Leo, I didn't mean that you wouldn't make a great father. Of course you would. You're easy-going and kind. You're reliable and intelligent. You would be amazing.' She shook her head. 'But you're married to *me*.'

'Dara, if it wasn't for you I would still be going through life without a true purpose. Falling in love with you made me realize what is truly important in life. Three years ago if you had told me that I would want to spend the rest of my life living in this castle I would have laughed you out of the room.' He turned to her, taking both of her hands in his. 'But here I am. And this is the only place I want to be.'

'I can't be somebody's mother. I just can't.'

'Dara, did you ever stop and think that maybe it's okay not to be the perfect mother? Sometimes it's okay just to try your best. I mean, you're telling me that you're a workaholic, and yet the matron told me that you've been visiting the orphanage three times a week. That's a two-hour round trip, alone, while simultaneously running your own business, yes?'

Dara shrugged. 'I made the time.'

'Exactly. Because you care about this boy.' Leo stepped forward, grasping her hands in his. 'Dara, I went to that orphanage today because I wanted to understand you. So that I could make you happy.' He paused for a moment. 'I honestly had no idea of the effect it would have on me. I suppose that somewhere in the back of my mind I've always worried that being raised by parents like mine meant that I could never be a good parent myself.'

'You would make a wonderful father, Leo,' Dara said softly.

'I'm not so sure about *wonderful*. But after today I know I would like the opportunity to try.'

Dara looked up into her husband's eyes and saw the

emotion there. 'Are you saying that you want us to start a family together?'

'We've been a family from the moment you agreed to spend the rest of your life as my wife. I want to take this next step with you—to start a new adventure.'

Dara closed her eyes, letting the air finally whoosh into her lungs. The fear of even daring to want this had stopped her from acknowledging her true feelings about Luca. Hearing Leo say these things… Hearing him shine a proverbial light on her deepest yearnings…

She looked up at her husband once more and saw that he was watching her quietly.

'I want to be Luca's mother.'

The words came out rushed and tumbled over each other on their way. But once she had said them out loud it was as though she truly understood herself for the first time. Her hands started to shake—a quake that continued up her arms and down into her abdomen.

Leo put his arms around her but she gently removed them, needing to pace for a moment with this newfound sense of terror coursing through her. It was one thing to be afraid of wanting something that she knew could never happen. But to admit that she wanted it…? To open herself to rejection and heartbreak…?

To Leo this was a new feeling—the idea of becoming a parent. But for Dara this was a sensation that had haunted her for years, a thought that had consumed her at times. She had fought back against the feelings of hopelessness by cutting the thought out of her life altogether and deciding that she no longer wanted to become a mother.

Now she knew the truth. She had never stopped wanting it. She had just been waiting for this moment.

'I can't believe this is happening…' Dara breathed, her thoughts swimming with the enormity of what they were discussing.

'It's only happening if you want it to.' Leo stood in front of her. 'I meant what I said on that beach three years ago. You will always be enough for me, Dara. You are more than I deserve.'

Dara felt the fear melt away as Leo's arms enveloped her, and all her worries seemed smaller all of a sudden. She breathed in the familiar scent of his aftershave and told herself that she needed to commit this perfect moment to memory.

'I want to start a family with you.' She pulled back to look into her husband's eyes. 'I want us to become Luca's parents. If he'll have us, that is.'

'Hearing him speak about you today, I have no doubt that he thinks just as much of you as you do of him,' Leo assured her.

'I hope so.' Dara bit her lip. 'Leo, once we take this step there is no going back. There will be no more impromptu trips to Paris—no more yachting for weeks along the Riviera. We'll have to consider school term times. It won't be just you and I.'

'I'm quite aware that children are a lot of responsibility.'

'I just want to make sure that you're certain this is what you want. That we aren't going into this with our eyes closed.'

'Dara, stop worrying and let yourself enjoy this. I have complete faith that you will plan every little detail perfectly. Just leave all the fun stuff to me.' He laughed.

Dara smiled. He was right—she was a ball of nerves.

She took a deep breath, feeling a sense of excited anticipation hum through her veins.

'I will start proceedings in the morning.' Leo smiled. 'We can go to the orphanage ourselves.'

'I can hardly believe that this is happening.' Dara shook her head. 'Never in my wildest dreams…'

Leo pressed his lips tenderly to hers, his hands spanning her waist and pulling her to him in a tight embrace. 'I was afraid to share you with anyone else, but now I find myself wanting to show you off to the world. You amaze me with all you've overcome.'

'You're the one who helped me to overcome it.'

Their kiss turned from soft to heated, and the wind whipped around them as the sun dipped slowly towards the sea.

The next morning Dara arrived at the orphanage bright and early, with her husband by her side. They entered the common room just as the children had finished breakfast. No sooner had they stepped into the room than a tiny head of jet-black curls came barrelling towards them.

'Do you know the yo-yo man?'

Luca's eyes widened as he looked from Dara to Leo. Dara imagined her husband must look like a giant from the small boy's height, and yet he wasn't frightened.

'Luca, this is my husband Leo. He came here to meet you.'

The other children had filtered into the room, all their attention on the man with the yo-yo. Leo continued to delight the children with more tricks and Luca sat resolutely by his side, telling all the other children that 'the yo-yo man' had come to meet him.

Before they knew it, the children were called to have lunch. As much as Dara wanted to stay there all day, she knew that now it was time for the official part of their visit.

As the lunch bell rang Luca's eyes turned wide and he ran to her. He looked up at her with that uncertain expression she had come to recognise so well after more than three months of visits.

'I promise that I will come back,' she said solemnly.

Luca was a child of abandonment, so he regularly made her promise that she was coming back in their same special way. Dara held out her pinkie finger, letting him lock it with his own tiny one.

She felt a hand at her waist. Leo stood by her side, watching the exchange with interest. 'Is this some secret handshake I don't know about?' he joked.

'I can teach it to you too,' Luca said quietly.

As Dara watched, her husband got down on his knees and promised the young boy that he would return. She felt a swell of love for this man who had helped her to overcome so much.

Leo straightened, and they waved as the boys ran in single file towards the lunchroom. Luca was the smallest of the lot.

'It was so good of you both to visit us today.' The friendly matron smiled as she welcomed them into her office. 'I couldn't help but notice your interest in little Luca,' she said speculatively.

Dara turned to the woman, meeting her gaze. 'My visits here haven't been as selfless as I've made them out to be.'

'You are a very kind woman, Dara. I don't believe that you came here out of your own interests.'

'Maybe not at first, but it has definitely become that way.'

'I have watched your progress with Luca intently. You know his history. He came to us a very scared and lonely boy. Since your visits he has changed. He talks more with the other children…he is more confident. Your attention did that for him.' She smiled again.

Leo stepped forward, taking Dara's trembling hand in his own. 'My wife and I would like to start proceedings to adopt Luca.' He felt the enormity of the words as he spoke them.

The other woman's eyes lit up with emotion and joy. 'Oh, after yesterday and today I confess that I had started to hope. But our hopes get dashed here far too often.'

'Our intentions are genuine. We would like to become Luca's parents,' Dara said. 'We know that the process is long, but we believe he will be happy with us. That we can give him a good home.'

Tears filled the old matron's eyes as she took one of Dara's hands in her own. 'You have no idea how long I've been waiting for you to realise that, Signora Valente.'

Dara stood by the fireplace, straightening the stockings and biting her lip. Was she jumping the gun by adding one smaller stocking beside their own two? She worried at her bottom lip for a moment, before making a final sweep of the living room. Piles of gifts lay stacked under the tree, ready to be torn open by eager little hands. She had wrapped each box painstakingly in bright paper with intricate bows. She wanted to make today as special as it could possibly be.

'Dara, stop worrying. The place looks amazing.' Leo strode into the living room, his hair lightly ruffled from being outside. 'You're going to have to get used to less organisation around here.'

'I know. I'm just keeping busy.' She sighed.

'He'll be here soon. You'll be kept *very* busy for the weekend. Last chance… You're sure you don't want to hire a nanny?' He smiled mischievously.

'We will do just fine on our own.' Dara laughed as Leo swept her into his arms. 'He's just one little boy—how much work could he be?'

'I have feeling those are brave last words.'

She felt the excitement and the nerves coursing through him just as they did inside her. Leo pressed his mouth to hers softly, tracing the outline of her lips with own. She twined her fingers in the hair at the nape of his neck and sighed as he deepened the kiss, moulding his hands tightly to her waist. He shaped his body closely against hers, the warmth of him pressing hard against her.

She wanted to remember this moment for ever. Kissing the man she loved, here, in the home they had created, as they waited to welcome their son to his new home for the first time.

Their son.

In just a few moments she would officially be a mother. The realisation hit her like a freight train and she broke off their kiss just as the doorbell rang.

'Are you ready?'

Leo looked into her eyes, squeezing her hand tightly as they made their way to the entrance of the *castello.*

He smiled. 'I can't wait to see his face once he realises he's going to live in a real-life castle.'

Dara felt her nerves melt away as she saw the excited expression on Leo's face. Suddenly she just knew that everything was going to be wonderful from this moment on.

They opened the door to find their social worker helping Luca out of the car. His tiny face was turned up and he was looking at the *castello* with awe.

Dara ushered Luca inside, welcoming the social worker, who would be staying for the settling-in period. The adoption process had definitely been speeded up by Leo, with the Valente name seeming to cut through some of the red tape, but it was far from over. This weekend was for Luca—to ensure that he was happy to come and live with them at the *castello* for good. They had a multitude of activities planned and had put the finishing touches to his bedroom.

Over the past weeks they had spent long hours bonding with the young boy, going on day trips and meeting with various officials. It was a gruelling process, but one that was vital. Everyone had to be sure that he was happy to be adopted by them. That was what mattered most.

Luca ran into the hall and barrelled into Leo's arms. 'Wow, you really *do* live in a castle!'

'I don't tell lies.' Leo smiled down at him.

'Will we be living here all the time?' he asked Dara in a small voice.

Dara looked at the social worker, aware that her every move was being assessed. 'If you would like it, this would be our home, yes.' She turned to Leo, feeling her confidence begin to falter.

'Are there ghosts in this castle?' Luca asked suddenly.

'There used to be.' Leo looked pointedly at Dara for a moment. 'But then a brave princess came and chased all the ghosts away.'

Dara felt tiny fingers wrap around her own. She looked down to see that Luca had grabbed on to her hand tightly as they ascended the stairs to show him his new bedroom. Her heart soared at this show of affection.

'I thought the knight was supposed to save the princess?' Dara questioned light-heartedly as she gripped her son's hand.

'Sometimes the knight is the one who needs to be saved.'

Leo caught her eye and Dara smiled to herself.

They had saved one another. Two broken souls who had somehow managed to make each other whole again. After all they had overcome in both their pasts, she was certain that the future could only be bright.

* * * * *

COMING NEXT MONTH FROM

Available October 20, 2015

#3377 A CHRISTMAS VOW OF SEDUCTION

Princes of Petras

by Maisey Yates

With one band of gold, Prince Andres of Petras can erase his past—and most pleasurable—sins. But his prospective bride is untamable Princess Zara. So the playboy prince must seduce her into compliance and crown her by Christmas!

#3378 THE SHEIKH'S CHRISTMAS CONQUEST

The Bond of Billionaires

by Sharon Kendrick

As the snow falls, innocent Olivia Miller finds a darkly handsome and compelling man on her doorstep. The sheikh she refused has arrived to whisk her off to his kingdom...and this time he *won't* take no for an answer!

#3379 UNWRAPPING THE CASTELLI SECRET

Secret Heirs of Billionaires

by Caitlin Crews

Lily Holloway turned her back on the forbidden passion she shared with Rafael Castelli five years ago. But when their paths cross again, Lily attempts to veil herself with deception in order to retain her freedom...and her child!

#3380 A MARRIAGE FIT FOR A SINNER

Seven Sexy Sins

by Maya Blake

Zaccheo Giordano is a man with one thing on his mind: revenge. And he'll start with his ex-fiancée, Eva Pennington. She *will* wear Zaccheo's ring again and he'll ensure their marriage will be real in *every* sense...

HPCNM1015RA

#3381 LARENZO'S CHRISTMAS BABY

One Night With Consequences

by Kate Hewitt

After two years behind bars, Larenzo Cavelli is determined to get his life back...starting with Emma Leighton. It was deception that imprisoned him, so what will happen when he discovers Emma's secret? One he might never be able to forgive...

#3382 BRAZILIAN'S NINE MONTHS' NOTICE

Hot Brazilian Nights!

by Susan Stephens

Chambermaid Emma Fane thinks her best friend's wedding will be the perfect distraction...until she spies Lucas Marcelos—father to her unborn child! It only took one night to change their lives, now they have nine months to face the consequences.

#3383 SHACKLED TO THE SHEIKH

Desert Brothers

by Trish Morey

Nanny Tora Burgess eagerly waits to meet her new boss—but is horrified to discover he's her red-hot, one-night lover! Rashid is cold, distant and has a shocking proposal that will shackle her to the sheikh forever!

#3384 BOUGHT FOR HER INNOCENCE

Greek Tycoons Tamed

by Tara Pammi

Jasmine Douglas is the only one who knows the darkness of Dmitri Karegas's past. But only Dmitri can help when she's forced to put her virginity up for sale. Now he must decide what to do with her...and her innocence!

SPECIAL EXCERPT FROM

Playboy Prince Andres of Petras is bound by royal duty and must finally pay the price for his past sins—by marrying the lost princess of Tirimia. From fiery passion to sinfully seductive kisses, is this one Christmas gift the prince will be keeping...forever?

Read on for a sneak preview of
A CHRISTMAS VOW OF SEDUCTION,
the first book in ***PRINCES OF PETRAS****,*
the sensational new duet by
USA TODAY *bestselling author* Maisey Yates.

She looked down, caught the glitter of her engagement ring on the hand that was squeezing him. Then she looked back up at his face. A mistake.

She barely had a chance to register the hot, angry glitter in his dark eyes before he closed the distance between them, his mouth crashing down onto hers.

The force of him pushing her back against the wall crushed their bodies together as he angled his head and slipped his tongue between her lips.

He proved then what he'd said before. He had the power. She could do nothing, not in this moment. Nothing but simply surrender to the heat coursing through her, to the electrical current crackling over her skin with a kind of intensity she'd never even imagined existed.

His hands were firm and sure on her hips, his body pressing her to the wall as he sought restitution for her attempt at claiming control.

HPEXP1015

"You want a fight?" He growled the words against her mouth. "I can give you a fight, Princess. We don't have to do this the easy way." He angled his head, parting his lips from hers, kissing her neck. She shivered, fear and arousal warring for pride of place inside her. "But if you want to test me, you have to be prepared for the results. I do not know what manner of man you have been exposed to in the past, but I am not one that can be easily manipulated."

He rocked his hips against hers, showing her full evidence of the effect she was having on his body. She had spent so much of her life being ignored that eliciting such a powerful response from such a man gratified her in ways she never could have anticipated.

She didn't know a kiss could be so many different things. That it could serve so many purposes. That it could make her feel hot, cold, afraid, enraptured. But it did. It was everything, and nothing she should ever have allowed to happen between them.

HPEXP1015